ESSENCE BESTSELLING AUTHOR

ANTHONY WHYTE

THIN
LINE

A CHILD'S EYES NEVER LIE

TEENLIT
Ages 12 Up

© 2013 Augustus Publishing, Inc.

PAPER BACK ISBN: 978-0982541524
EBOOK ISBN: 978-1935883289

Novel by Anthony Whyte
Edited by Parijat Deasai
Creative Direction & Design by Jason Claiborne
Cover Illustration by Marthalicia Matarrita

Augustus Publishing paperback June 2013
www.augustuspublishing.com

Dedicated to the Lion of Inwood…

Will Alicea

Your bravery astounds even me

My brother

Your kindness guides me

Will Teez

Your memory lives on forever

always

RIP

You'll never be forgotten…

ANTHONY WHYTE

ACKNOWLEDGEMENTS

It takes a village to raise a child... That being said, I'd like to thank all who've helped to put this book together. Tracy Sherrod for planting the idea, my niece, Yolanda Palmer for the expert rewrite, Professor Menaukha Case @Empire State College for the cuts... Parijat Desai Editor, Amicus Editing for edits. Marthalicia Matarrita for her painting skills, Shulamy Casado, great work... Jason Claiborne for orchestrating... Congratulations to Lebron James on being the MVP in winning his first championship with the Miami Heat. To all the readers who requested a book their children could read... A Thin Line... No cursing!

ANTHONY WHYTE

PROLOGUE

It was seven in the morning when two black unmarked cars rolled to a stop outside the most pristine house on the quiet, tony block. The fog of the fall proved thick enough to hide the moving figures in the shadows. Five immaculately dressed men jumped out of the cars clothed in dark suits, and equipped with automatic weapons by their sides. With precise discipline, the men quickly moved into the shield of darkness and settled into hidden positions waiting for their cue.

7:15 a.m. Lolo and her father walked out of their front door, as they usually did on her school days. The black Mercedes Benz with diplomatic tags was already purring. Steve Mozi always started the car with his remote control so the interior of the car would be warm and welcoming, and he did no different on this cool, misty spring morning. Lolo and her father rushed to the inviting car while unknown to them, danger lurked. Lolo turned to wave good-bye to her mother who was waving at her to come back inside.

"Lolo, you forgot your lunch," Mrs. Mozi shouted.

Yatzi Mozi came running behind them to greet her daughter with a turkey and cheese sandwich prepared with motherly love. Suddenly she recognized the cold stares on the strange men's faces. Her mouth opened but Mrs. Mozi's shriek didn't come fast enough. The chilling whistle of silencers from guns aimed at her only daughter and husband killed her sound. Bullets flew and Mrs. Mozi realized too late what was taking place.

"Oh God, Lolo, Steve, look out…!" She shrieked in fear.

Her cry came way too late. Yatzi Mozi ran out of the mansion toward her husband and daughter, and she too became part of the melee. The assassins continued their charge at the unsuspecting family members, tactically gunning all of them down.

It was a twenty after seven. Eleven-year-old Lolo, her father Steve Mozi, and her mother, Yatzi, were caught in the shooting gallery without any cover or concealment. In a savage onslaught of lead, the family was brutally murdered.

Three of the men quickly checked the dead bodies. One grabbed the attaché case Steve Mozi had been carrying. Racing back to the cars, they jumped in and quickly slammed the doors. Tires screeched as the two cars peeled off, alerting the attention of a neighbor. At twenty five after seven, the disturbed neighbor notified the police.

7:45 a.m. Mrs. Rita Sanchez, a young Puerto Rican woman, was hurrying out of her front door, followed by her son Shareef. This mother-and-child pair lived in a beautiful house on a block located in the Riverdale section of the Bronx. They lived at the end of the block. Though only six huge houses away from the Mozi home, they were completely unaware of what had taken place there twenty-five minutes earlier.

"C'mon, Shareef, you've got to hurry—it's already seven forty-five. You're going to be late for school if you don't move livelier," Rita said to her eleven-year-old son, following slowly behind her.

"Okay mom," Shareef grumbled, rubbing his eyes.

"You were up late again, weren't you?"

"I went to sleep after the game…"

"Just as I thought. You were up watching basketball and did not get enough sleep."

"But it was the playoffs, mom."

"And so what? Well, you're going to stay awake, and don't even let me hear that you were sleeping in class."

"Okay mom," Shareef yawned.

"That's what you get for staying up all night and watching basketball. I told you to go to sleep early, boy. "

"I…ah was in bed…and I…" Shareef said, fumbling for an answer.

"Sure you were. Get in the car and fasten your seatbelt, Shareef," she said.

By the time she guided the Volvo out of her driveway, Shareef's eyes were already closed. As Rita Sanchez drove by the home of the wealthiest family in the neighborhood, she saw the yellow tape draped around the front of the home, and the police cars and detectives moving about. The area was cordoned off and was now officially a crime scene.

What had gone wrong? Rita wondered, slowing to rubberneck at the commotion in the peaceful neighborhood. She knew the immigrant family—consisting of mother, who was an immigration lawyer, and father, a diplomat at the U.N. Shareef and their daughter not only attended the same school, but they were also best friends. Her face was flushed with concern as she slowed. The crime scene was too much for the curious Rita Sanchez. Her son dozed while she got out the car and curiously consulted with an officer on the scene.

"Good morning—what's wrong?" she asked, showing her badge.

"Triple murder…" he answered, glancing at her badge momentarily and nodding.

"Oh my…" Rita exhaled, as the body bags were zipped. "I didn't hear a thing out of the normal."

"It looks like a pretty well-organized hit. The killers must have used silencers. Did you know the family?"

"My son goes to the same school as their daughter. Was she…?"

"They got everyone. She won't be attending school—hey do me a favor, when you get to the school…"

"Okay, I'll be glad to help in anyway I can."

"Maybe you can give the principal my card," he said, handing a business card to Rita.

"Oh my gosh! Speaking of school! My son is gonna be late."

"Is that him sleeping in the car? Please don't mention this to anyone just yet."

"Yes, just as well. Lolo was his good friend. I don't want him to know about this right now. Oh God, this is soo horrible!" Rita exclaimed in grief.

With her arms hugging her fall jacket, Rita Sanchez had a gnawing feeling in her stomach. On shaky legs, she walked back, staring at Shareef fast asleep in the waiting car.

CHAPTER 1

The Night Before

"This cannot be happening!" I exclaimed.

Here I was dressed in my lucky, throwback jersey cheering on my favorite team, the Cavaliers. The name of the team captain, James, embroidered in big letters across the back and his number 23 plastered across the center. I was stunned as the final eastern conference playoff game came to an end.

"No! I can't believe it. They really lost. I have been

defeated. I just knew we would win the championship," I uttered under my breath.

I stared at the television like the game had not ended. Maybe I was expecting the score to change, but it didn't. I shook my head, still not believing that the Cavs were booted from the playoffs.

My cell phone already began to ring. I didn't even have to check the caller ID. My best friend, Lolo, was ready to talk me out of my misery. Right then I was quite irritable and cranky and really didn't feel like talking to my antagonist, but I answered.

"Hello Lolo," I said, plopping down hard on my bed with my elbows resting on soft pillows.

James, the Cavaliers, I already felt it coming, and knew I shouldn't have picked up her call, but Lolo can really be persistent. She probably would have just kept on calling until I answered. Then she'd chewed me out for ignoring her. My television was still on, and in the break during the post-game interview. I listened to Lolo's ideas about solving world hunger. Who cares about world hunger? My team lost! My world's shattered, and tomorrow I'll have to face the jeers from my classmates.

The sports channel replayed footage of the game for an

agonizing eternity while Lolo chatted my head off with ideas for saving the human race. Sports reporters anxiously awaited answers. James, still looking regal, tried to answer the reporters' questions as humbly as possible.

"...We'll take the L as a learning experience. Next time we're in the play-offs we won't be new, and this loss will prepare us for the future..."

I just couldn't watch anymore, so I turned the television off, brooding. My favorite team along with my favorite player was officially done for the season. Worst of all, I had bragged to everyone at school that the Cavs was about to win their first NBA title. How was I supposed to know their center would go down with an injury?

"This team is a good team but tonight our opponent was better and we'll have to regroup and be ready next year," James continued. *"This loss really hurts...*

I looked at the television still shaking my head in disbelief, and heard Lolo said, "It's your loss, Shareef." She spoke quietly in her proper way of speaking. "I'm going to be famous one day, but not from playing any sports. I'll be famous for helping others less fortunate," she explained.

I listened uninterested knowing her folks had loads of

money. Lolo's father was a high-priced lawyer and advisor to diplomats. Her mother worked for the same law firm in immigration. She made a lot of money representing foreign consumers and businesses. Lolo and her mother along with an assortment of relatives lived in the largest house on the block. She could afford to talk about helping others.

On any given day there would be six or seven Mercedes Benzes competing for parking in the three-car garage. There was a constant stream of foreign dignitaries stopping by for well-orchestrated dinners and cocktails. Lolo had explained the various diplomatic license plates to me. Her parents were international citizens and Lolo could think on a universal level. Meanwhile, my family was considered working class.

My stepfather Stanley McCoy-Sanchez was a schoolteacher and my mother Rita Sanchez was a police officer. There was one car in the garage and my parents complained about having to work all the time to pay their bills. Stanley's father died leaving him the modest house in that exclusive neighborhood, which we could have never afforded ourselves. Lolo was really my only friend so I usually tried to entertain her, but tonight I am just not in the mood. She kept on yakking, but I knew that this was her way of cheering me up.

"Oh Lolo, don't try to make me feel better," I said, sulking.

"I know you feel bad about Lebron James, but I think next season will be better…"

"Aw, get off it, Lolo. You're only trying to make me feel better."

"Well, isn't that what friends are supposed to do? What would make you happy?" she asked.

I took a minute thinking of the right comeback. Finally, I thought of a clever answer.

"Okay, if you really want to know what will make me happy, you could take me to see the new *Batman* movie on Saturday."

"I don't think I can do that. Saturday is when this stupid police officer usually brings his daughter over here while he and my father play pool in the den. But Sunday I am definitely free…" Lolo answered.

"I have to go on Saturday…"

"What's the big deal about Saturday, Shareef?"

"'Cause I'm going to see my grandmother on Sunday, that's why. Now please, Lolo. I really gotta get some sleep before my mom starts yelling at me again."

"Oh Shareef, you're such a sleepyhead…"

"I'm not…"

"You're so too…"

"I'm only this way because the Cavs ah…"

"Fact remains you're a sleepyhead. How many times have I had to wake you up in class? I swear at times you are just asking for trouble. You know Ms. Brown already has it in for you…" Lolo said, interrupting.

"She only has it in for me because my parents can't afford to treat her to big Christmas ski trips and tours of Martha's Vineyard."

"That may be true. Privilege is definitely the way to her heart, but you should not make yourself an easy target either."

"Goodnight, Lolo. This sleepyhead wants to go to bed," I said, interrupting. I didn't want to have to face the inevitable teasing and jeering that tomorrow's day at school would bring any earlier than I had to.

"Shareef, remember it's only a game. There are more important things in life than basketball."

"You could be right, Lolo. But right now basketball is the most important thing in my life."

"What about world hunger and children dying of diseases

in Africa, Thailand, South America?"

"Lolo, it's not time yet for me to think about things like that. That's adult stuff."

"You've got to start somewhere, someday."

"We'll start that when we go to college. And I'm a long way off from that. Thank God," I said sleepily.

"Shareef, you promise? Say you promise," Lolo was persistent.

"Okay, I promise we'll do something that will help stop world hunger," I said reluctantly.

"Oh, we could start a wonderful organization that will benefit all of humankind. Of course we are going to need money. We could throw a party and invite all the richest people to donate money and…" Lolo said excitedly.

"Lolo, Lolo, please can we talk about this at school tomorrow?"

"Of course. You'll see this is something great. I'm gonna get on the computer and start contacting different organizations for grants and…"

"Ah, okay. Maybe we could start planning tomorrow."

"Okay alright, sleepyhead. Don't be late for school tomorrow. You'll see all the work I've already done and…"

"Lolo, tomorrow I'll see you."

"Okay, I can't wait to see you tomorrow. Together I know we can really make a difference, Shareef."

"Fine, we'll continue this tomorrow. Lolo, I've got to get some sleep already."

I finally put the phone down. Why did I rush her off the phone? It's not like I can sleep anyway. I could call her back, but she would just talk me to death anyway. I closed my eyes and was as still as I could, trying to quiet the thoughts swirling through my head. I looked at the clock it was already five in the morning. I had just acquired the unattainable. Then before I knew it, the alarm sounded. It felt like I never slept at all. Red-eyed and tired, I stood in front of the bathroom mirror nodding off, as I got dressed for school.

"Hurry up, Shareef. You haven't eaten your breakfast yet."

"Okay, mommy. I'll be there in one second."

"That's all the time you'll have if you don't come down right now, Shareef."

From the time at the breakfast table to leaving the house, all I kept thinking about was the loss. I had to attend school. My classmates were not going to let me live this down. I had showed off in front of them and picked the wrong team to win the championships.

"C'mon, Shareef, buckle up," my mother said, and waved at my stepfather leaving for work. "Have a great day, Stanley."

I nodded politely at him, but was preoccupied with thinking of how challenging the sixth grade was, especially in a new school. I had gone to war against half the school, and now my team was out.

"Have a nice day, Shareef."

Mother's voice snatched me out of my thoughts, and into the reality of facing jeers from my classmates.

"Hey you lil' squirt," the school bully, Bobby McNeil yelled at me in the lunchroom.

He was taller, stronger and bigger than everyone at school. He was really good at everything athletic, as well as fighting, picking on others, and running his mouth. And today, his sights were set on me. He never paid attention in class and couldn't wait for lunch to start clowning.

"Hey you, chump. Stop ignoring me. You're acting like you didn't hear. What happened to Lebron James and that team of—lo-o-o-sers? Losers!"

He was shouting, and now everyone noticed. His voice

echoed louder as they laughed. He had called my favorite team losers but I did not want beef with this guy. He could beat anyone in the school easily and had proved that on many occasions.

Rumors were that his parents had money and were able to donate enough to the privately funded school to buy away any punishment for his bad behavior. My mother struggled to send me to this school. She wanted the 'best education' for me. I was her only child and she did everything to make my life the best possible.

She said she never wanted me to turn out like my real father, Tyrell Greene. She would say, "I don't want you to be like that no-good bum." That was her pet name for him since she never actually called him by his name. According to my mother, deep down inside, he was a great man with a warm heart, but his temper and foul mouth ruined what could have been. She would say he was like a Kandinsky, a two-sided painting. On one side he was charming, handsome, intelligent and loving provider who loved us with all the breath in his body. And on the other, he was a drunk who would get mad and lash out at who ever dared cross his path. He never expressed his rage toward mom or me, but did enough to spend weekends in jail. The time he spent in and out of jail would only prove to make him tougher.

Despite his record, it was always easy for him to get work because when he cleaned up, he was a loveable guy. He worked construction and would show me how to fix things and do 'man's work', as he would call it. When he had money, he would buy me anything I wanted. When there was no work, he could not afford to pay a single dollar of child support. One thing was for sure, he wanted me to be tough. And he would not have allowed me to take any lip from this bully or anyone for that matter.

I remember one Sunday afternoon when he shoved some young dude who was trying to cut the line at the movies. We were standing on line waiting to go to the movies and some boys were trying to cut the line. The four of them stood around talking and when they thought no one was watching, one of them would jump in the line.

They did this all the way up to where my dad and I were standing, close to the theater entrance. When the boy tried to sneak on the line, I saw him then alerted Dad. My father shoved the guy so hard the poor fool landed about a hundred feet away. Then my dad beat up the others, all while giving his usual lecture on the path to world peace.

"See what I'm talking about, Shareef? Everyone picks

on the soft people. They get pushed around. The strong people—
we get our respect."

Other patrons who were close enough to hear him made
faces of disgust.

"How could that man beat on those poor kids like that?"

"They crossed the thin line between love and hate," my
father answered.

He joined his fists side by side and raised them forward.
Onlookers saw words tattooed on his fingers. *LOVE* was spelled
out on each finger of his right hand, and *HATE,* in a similar
fashion, on his left.

The buzz circulated the theater and pretty soon everyone
was talking about it. I often wonder why he was my father. I
could see what mother told me attracted to her: his raw, rugged,
handsome face. He also had a terrible temper to go with it. But I
never thought of settling anything first with my fist.

Today in the lunchroom, I ignored the bully's needling.
His silly words won't do me any harm, was the mantra I used. I
felt my eyes burning, and knew that I was already too tired for
his nonsense. I allowed myself to glance up from my tasteless
bologna and cheese sandwich, to look around for my best friend,
Lolo. She was nowhere in sight. Maybe she had stayed in the

classroom to help her teacher, as she often did.

Our families were not only neighbors, but also best friends, and we attended the same school. She had my favorite PlayStation games. Best of all, she trusted me with them—I mean she let me hold onto four or five games at a time.

Once we met, Lolo and I quickly became really good friends. It was the first time that I had a girl for a close friend.

"What happened to your team, huh Shareef?"

"They left their hearts in the locker room…"

"No they left their balls in the locker room," another classmate interjected and the joke raged on.

And on it went, at my expense. Soon it was mounting to a crescendo of uncontrollable, raucous laughter. I hated being the butt of their jokes and tried to excuse myself from their graciousness. Raising my hand, I walked over to where the lunchroom teacher was standing. She was in the midst of scolding another student when I approached. Her makeup cracked when she spoke. I could tell Miss Brown was in her evilest mood.

"Miss Brown, I would like to be excused."

"Excuse me, young man. What do you say before you disturb someone like myself?"

It was apparent not only to me, but to anyone else close

enough to hear what her answer to my request would be. I knew immediately from the way she squinted.

"That is certainly not the way you were taught in this school to speak, mister."

It was clear she was putting me through the motions. I swallowed hard and summoned my determination to make another attempt.

"Excuse me, Miss Brown. May I be excused from the lunchroom? I would like to use the boys' room."

I waited several haunting seconds while she rolled her eyes at me. Finally she opened her mouth and answered.

"No, Shareef. You always want to go somewhere. Go back and finish with your lunch," she loudly said.

I could hear the chuckling. It was then that I realized how much I hated Miss Brown. I knew she had no love for me. But Lolo had always liked her, and they shared a connection that I never understood.

"Thank you," I muttered, and went back to my seat.

When I reached my table I saw what look like pee where I once sat. I glared. No one moved; there was only a roar of laughter. It was Bobby. He had poured apple juice on my seat to make it look like I peed on myself.

Bobby was always playing stupid pranks on everyone. If only Lolo was here, she would tell me how to deal with this situation. She always did. Where was she? I wondered looking at my classmates, seemingly enjoying the school bully's wisecracks.

"Aw, did you pee on yourself? Loser…loser…" I heard him, but ignored the taunting. "Oh man, you're not trying to run, are you? Take it like a man. Don't try to run like a punk, loser."

He was on a roll and his comments brought him another round of laughter. The whole school feared him. He was not saying anything funny, but students laughed themselves silly as he ranted on to avoid being the next object of his attention. I kept my mouth shut and wondered about Lolo.

Maybe she was out starting that organization of hers to fight hunger. She was crazy and was probably out recruiting other helpers. Although she tended to be a little eccentric, Lolo was the smart, go-getter type who wouldn't wait for me. She probably did not really need school. But who needed school anyway?

These kids were a bunch of show-offs. They irked me, but since I met Lolo, it was easier to cope with them. As I glanced around the lunchroom, I saw that they were actually scared.

"Okay, Shareef, you've been disruptive enough for the day. Please sit."

It was Miss Brown flapping her lips and coming at me like I was the culprit.

"But someone...like put this—" I started, but she didn't let me finish.

"Young man you will clean up the mess and sit down!" She ordered gruffly.

"It's not my mess! I got up and—"

"It's your seat, your chair, and your mess to clean up!" Miss Brown said harshly.

My palms started to sweat and I bit my lips, determined not to cry as I felt the anger stirring inside me. I stared at the mess on the seat.

"Now you clean that mess or you will be getting a demerit. And remember, you are only one demerit away from suspension."

Miss Brown had a reputation for giving suspensions to the poor and scholarship kids like me without batting an eye. I knew she would call my mom and complain to the principal until I was finally expelled for good. As much as I hated this school, I knew what graduation from here meant to my mom.

She was always telling me how graduating from a good school like this would pay off in the end with top picks for prep schools and college. I didn't want the trouble so I took a deep breath, picked up a napkin and wiped the mess from the chair.

"Now sit down!" She ordered.

I complied. Dutifully I sat, feeling as vexed as I could get. My mind was in a panic and sought someone to blame. This was all Lolo's fault. The thought spread through my cerebellum and became a prominent diversion. Lolo was my only protection from this private-school madness, being that she was a true friend, and had also come from money, they treated her different. Miss Brown would be more reserved around her. As I stared at the back of Miss Brown, I thought she was probably smiling as she walked away. I felt like cursing but held my tongue. Instead I grimaced like she had used pepper-spray on me. I really wanted to ask her what was nice about her, but didn't.

There were so many thoughts going through my mind all at once, I felt like screaming. But I had no one to scream at. My feelings didn't seem to matter so I put them aside and thought about Lolo.

Over the past two years, it was hard to believe, but as far as I recalled she had never missed school. Today was the exception. Of course Lolo had to be out on the day I needed her most. I tried to ride out Bobby's taunting, until he walked up and slapped me in the back of my head. My hair was freshly cut, so the slap stung. Milliseconds before I could even think to retaliate, Miss Brown was on the scene and to his rescue.

"Stop that right this minute. The both of you...!" She yelled.

That thin line had been crossed. And now I refused to back down like I was a chump.

"You try that again, punk. I ain't one of these private-school chumps. I'm not afraid of you..." I started as the bully jumped in my face.

"Yeah, you wanna try and back that brave talk up? I own this school. You think 'cause you a black Rican from public school you can fight me?"

He was too close for me to retreat. I bit my lip knowing that casualty was expected. I was about to build up enough courage to swing when Miss Brown was on my back.

"Shareef! Shareef, you stop that foul-mouth cursing and get over there on the line now!" She screamed.

"He started with me. I swear he did."

She turned away, ignoring me and said, "Boys and girls,

lets get our things together. It's time to leave the lunchroom in an orderly fashion. Shareef, you get over here, now!" Miss Brown barked.

Miss Brown probably goes home and transforms into the evilest of witches, I was thinking as I took my place in the line.

Though I tried not to brood over what had happened in the lunchroom for the rest of the school day, I did. I mean I couldn't concentrate and time seemed to move slowly. Finally the sound of the bell rang and it seemed the torture was over.

I could get home play some *NBA Live* and tell Lolo about my crazy day. I'd find out why she missed school. I couldn't wait to talk to her. She was always going on about the importance of being in school—now I'd get her for sure. The day ended with me smiling at the opportunity.

Barely dodging Miss Brown flying past on the broomstick I imagined, I waited for my mother to come and get me from this wreck of a day. I glimpsed the car and sprinted across the schoolyard to her.

"Hi Shareef," she said. Her smile was faint. I kissed her and she patted my head.

"Hi, Mommy, how're you?"

There was no need for her to answer. The serious

expression she now wore on her face said it all. Bad news traveled fast. I had to formulate a plan.

"Mommy, it wasn't my fault. I…" I started, but was quickly cut-off.

"Huh-uh," she said, shaking her head. "Shareef, please say nothing else to incriminate yourself."

Without another word, she grabbed my arm and we headed to the principal's office. I dragged my feet as much as possible while my stomach did cartwheels.

We came to the office and the principal was standing outside along with the witch. The principal motioned for me to wait outside. As my mother entered the office, I sat down apprehensively and waited.

Immediately I removed a textbook from my book bag and buried my head in it. Lolo had always told me this worked in case of emergency. The words blurred as I tried to focus on the text.

I was filled with anxiety and could not absorb a syllable. Miss Brown must have reported me to the principal and they had called my mother to inform her of their version of the story. All of a sudden the room shrank. I felt like I couldn't breathe. The walls were tumbling down on me. There was no use trying to concentrate on the text. I hated school. I scratched my head, seething.

Later my mother emerged from the office wearing a grim expression. I couldn't immediately see her anger. Instead of the lecture, she signaled for me to follow to the exit. Staff members were looking at me pitifully as we walked by.

"Mom," I said, when I had caught up to her.

"Yes, Shareef," she answered.

I was confused by the patience in her tone. Completely thrown for a loop, my thoughts reshuffled. Mother was really in a weird mood. That witch Miss Brown was to be blamed for all of this. She had hypnotized my mother and charged me with false story.

I could tell by the way she gripped my hand walking to the car something was wrong. Mother appeared to be under a spell that either made her scared or so angry she was afraid to lose her temper. She waited for me to buckle my seat belt. I was a little worried.

"Mom, are you mad at me or…?"

I glanced at her and realized that she was staring at me really hard. It was as if she was trying to sum up my fate. If I'm lucky, there'll be no video games for a week, or no phone privileges. I won't be able to talk to Lolo. That wasn't good, but at least I'd be able to e-mail her. I was thinking the worst, when suddenly mother hugged me and tears welled in her eyes. I didn't understand.

Maybe dad was arrested again. He was drunk a lot, causing a ruckus and getting tossed in jail every week or so. Mother always had to bail him out. She would be sad for about two or three days and then she would be back to normal. Once she arrested a kid she told me that reminded her of me. Mother almost had a nervous breakdown and would greet me each day with an emotional hug.

When I first joined the school, I had wanted no part of it. But after meeting Lolo, I coped better. Mother was happy to know she lived on our block. Her family was rich, and that seemed to take my mind and my mother's off the episode when she arrested the kids. Mom wasn't as emotional. Most of all, I was happy Lolo and her parents lived in the largest house.

At a party they invited us to; my parents met her parents. They liked each other. Pretty soon my stepfather, Stanley McCoy and Lolo's father became great friends. Both were interested in education and Mr. Mozi always contributed generously to Stanley's school causes.

Mr. Mozi also made great financial contributions to the school I attended. I guessed that's the reason Lolo got so much respect from the staff at school. I was thinking and staring back at the church-gray color of the huge school building as it became smaller in the rearview.

Mother paid close attention to the road. Every now and then she would glance at me and smile. It was a nervous smile, like she had just been caught in a lie. I was scared but still wanted to ask. The feeling of wanting to go to the bathroom came, and it caused great discomfort. I was getting nervous. What else could go wrong?

My thoughts took me on a journey. By the end, I decided that if she had done something wrong, I would be able to forgive her—she was my mother.

"Mom, is everything alright?" I asked and held my breath. She didn't answer immediately. We reached a stoplight and she turned and examined me. "Well…"

"Do you have your seatbelt on properly?"

"Huh mom? I do. I do," I said somewhat frustrated. I thought she would let me have it.

My mother always let me know about everything. She told me of the time when my dad and her broke up. That was a very hard time in my life. My dad got drunk before picking me up from the park. The festival I was at ended hours before he made an appearance. It was the last time I saw him until he went to court. Mom had to go to the park police and plead for them not to report the incident. They did because my inebriated father had cursed a supervisor and had gotten a lot of people mad.

It led to her near suspension from the police training academy and disciplinary letter in her file. After that incident, I was sent to live with my grandmother.

When she completed her police training we moved in with her new boyfriend Stanley. He was a public schoolteacher and warned my mother to transfer me to private school. All of my friends attended public school so that was tough. After switching schools, I lost contact with them.

The kids at the old school were like me. Most were from working- or middle-class parents. They were from the same neighborhood, and they were into cigarettes, video games, music, and girls.

At the new school, they were all rich. Lolo and I were the only black kids, which meant we always seemed to stand out. The kids there were into international travel and music concerts, because they had the means to get anything they wanted.

Mother kept driving and I was trying figure out what the punishment would be. But she seemed sad, not mad. Maybe she was ashamed of my behavior at lunch. No, she loved me, and I didn't hit that bully. I glanced around to see if Miss Brown would zoom by us cackling in the wind.

"Mom, I don't think I like that school. I mean take for example… They all like different basketball teams than I do. Because the school bully likes the Celtics, then no one is allowed to talk about any other teams. Not for me," I said, shaking at my head and looking for her reaction.

She would talk about it now I was sure. If Lolo were here, she would have told her what had really happened.

"He started teasing me first," I said.

Because my mother was a police officer I felt that it was impossible to hide anything from her. She was always telling me that the police were trained to get the truth out of you so I figured it best to explain my role so that she would see the truth. Maybe she would not take away my privileges.

"Mom, see it's like this, ah… See…" I started and she gave me that motherly look. The unspoken was enough said.

"What is it, Shareef?"

"Well… See mom, Lebron and the Cavs had lost in the

play-offs and see I was hoping… Well telling everyone that the Cavs would win. I mean—they were up *at home* against the Celtics. Then they lost the final game, and the Celtics won the series. At school, they started teasing me, talking trash. I never answered back, mom. You'd be proud of me. I mean not that I didn't want to… He even called the team a bunch of faggots. Now that wasn't nice, but did I say anything back? No…"

Mother seemed ill at ease. Maybe she didn't believe my version of what happened. Miss Brown is such a witch, now she had my mother under her spell and I would certainly face punishment. I reached for the ace in the hole.

"Whatever Miss Brown said is a lie. If Lolo was here she would tell you what I'm saying is true."

I was almost shouting, but remembered how mother was always telling me that shouting doesn't make you right. I wished so badly that Lolo had been at school today.

The car noticeably sped up as we passed Lolo's house. I noticed the yellow tape. I felt my heart suddenly starting to race. What was wrong? By the time mother pulled to a stop, I saw tears in her eyes. What was going on? It was my turn to put the stare on her.

"Okay mother, you better level with me," I said,

mimicking her.

My mother smiled. Then she cried a little, and finally she hugged me closely.

"Oh my God, Shareef," she said, smothering me against her breast.

As I held her I could feel my mother's body trembling and a strange feeling overcame me, causing me to shudder. It was the fear of finding out something bad. There was a noticeable strain on my mother's face. I wanted to know why.

"Mommy, please tell me what's wrong," I pleaded.

I felt like crying without knowing why. Mom stared at me and started crying again holding me tightly. I knew something was very wrong, judging from the yellow tape. I hoped it had nothing to do with Lolo. She told me she never missed a day of school. Her voice kept replaying in my mind.

We were out of the car and mother still held on to me as if she was protecting me. But protecting me from what, and from whom? I couldn't take the suspense.

"It has to do with Lolo, and that's the reason you do not say what's going on?" I asked, and Mother hugged me.

I stared down the block. Everyone knew that plastic yellow tape is used to mark the scene of a crime.

CHAPTER 2

I stood frozen at the door as sweat trickled down my back, but could not remove my eyes from the scene. I could feel my mother pulling me inside, but was too engulfed in a flood of emotions. My hair stood on end when I realized that this was the first time I had seen yellow tape on this block, and I strained to see more. Turning to my mother I searched for an explanation but she was already walking toward the door. She entered the house and left the door open without looking back. I ran after her.

"Mom, what happened over at Lolo's?"

I had caught up to her. She placed her handbag and keys on the end table before looking at me. Again, I could see the tears welling in her eyes.

"Mommy, please tell me what happened?"

I was pleading but she said nothing. Then she reached for my hand. I placed my hand in hers and felt her trembling.

"Sometimes bad things happen to good people," she said.

I waited as she paused to let her tears out. All the time I kept wondering what was coming next. I knew whatever it was would be enough to change my young life for good, as I had never once witnessed my mother cry—not even when Dad was getting jailed on weekends.

Could thieves have broken in? Stolen valuable things? I did not recall seeing any of the cars outside. I tried being patient as mother gathered herself. I could only see pain in her eyes, and I feared the worst. I felt my stomach cramping. My mother glanced around before saying anything.

"Have a seat, son," she said, her voice straining with emotion.

Her words came in a whisper, and I did not know how to

react. I wanted to hurry my mother on, but there was something inside me telling me that I really did not want to hear what she had to say. Go upstairs, the voice inside me warned. My stomach tightened. Then Stanley walked in.

"Honey, the whole thing is on the news…" He started to speak, but saw me sitting next to my mother, and his mouth stopped moving.

He walked over to where we were in the family room. I shook my head when I heard what he said.

"Does he know?" He asked my mother like I was the invisible man.

I wanted to embarrass him the way the witch at school did me for being rude. Instead I looked at my distraught mother while she sobbed. Her shoulders were jerking with the force of her tears. It felt surreal. Maybe I was having a bad dream. My stepfather's fumbling pierced my consciousness when he resorted to his usual excuse to dismiss my curiosity.

"Shareef, excuse us, please. Your mother and I have something to talk about alone," he said.

I shot him my short, dirty look before leaving. If only my father were here, he would be speaking to me a whole lot differently. He would have never dared say anything to me in front of my real dad. I could feel their eyes on me.

"Shareef, start doing your homework," mother instructed.

I walked slowly to the refrigerator and got some juice. I was about to go upstairs to my room when my mother stopped me. She held my arm and said, "Honey, I think we should let Shareef know everything before…" Her voice trailed and I knew it was painful for her to continue.

"Now may not be the right time, sweetheart. He's still only a little boy!" Stanley objected. He was such a pee-hole. That's exactly what I felt like saying, but again, out of respect for my elders, I bit my lips. My mother looked at me pitifully. She had taught me well.

"Mom, I'm not a little boy. I'm almost twelve years old. I know that yellow tape around an area means a crime has been committed in there."

"I've got to censor those *CSI* movies. You're watching too many," she smiled and wiped at her tears.

"I don't think he should hear the official police details," Stanley said.

My stepfather paced nervously as he spoke. Mother seemed determined to let me know what was up. I sat down sipped the juice and listened attentively as she began.

"Shareef," she said, dabbing at her tears.

It made me sad to see my mother with tears running while my stepfather paced back and forth, occasionally glancing back at us.

"Ah sweetheart can you get me a glass of water?" she said to my stepfather. He walked to the kitchen. "Shareef, when we met the Mozis we were not aware… We did not know they were who they were."

Mother was apprehensive about revealing too much of the 'official police details' as Stanley had called it. Stanley brought her glass of cool water. He went back to his nervous pacing as my mother continued.

"Mr. Mozi worked as a diplomat, but failed to mention his lucrative side gig."

"What do you mean, lucrative side gig…?" I asked.

"It turned out that he was using his connections to launder money for some major international players," mother said, and I looked at her incredulously.

"Huh? Major, as in what? Mom, spit it out… What's going on?"

"Shareef, please listen. Mr. Mozi played a large role in embezzlement schemes and money-laundering operations that allowed mobsters to funnel drugs into the United States without having to be processed by the authorities," she said.

You could hear a pin drop. I stared at her as if she had suddenly lost her mind.

"What! No, that's not true—you're mistaken. Mom, what are you saying? C'mon mom, you know the Mozis. We've been to their house, to their parties, and I have never seen any drug dealers or mob guys. We saw city council members, senators, and even the mayor. They're all attorneys and doctors and…"

I waited for my mother's reaction. She had that look on her face that read, 'sorry Shareef, wrong answer'. I could not believe what I was hearing. The Mozis were the most prominent folks on the block, now my mom was calling them criminals. I listened intently as mom continued.

"The family has very good connections in the legitimate world, but they had secretly set up a drug ring and money-laundering scheme covering three continents."

The news hit me so hard, my mouth and hand opened. Suddenly I heard the glass with the juice crashing to the floor. My stepfather froze in his tracks, and mother shook her head.

"Mr. Mozi... Lolo's father…"

"Mom, I know Mr. Mozi is Lolo's father," I interrupted.

My stepfather glared while cleaning up the spillage.

"If you don't shut up and listen…" Mother warned.

"Mom, I'm sorry but I'm nervous."

"Nervous, why are you?"

"Mom, I really thought that it was about Lolo, but it's about her father," I said, trying to calm myself down.

I could feel my mother staring at me. I was up, about to excuse myself, but she held her hand up and stopped me.

"Wait a minute Shareef, there is more," she said and her voice sounded grave.

I sat back down and pursed my lips, waiting for the worse.

"Mr. Mozi was being investigated by the CIA, FBI, and local law enforcement. They had unmarked cars and followed him everywhere he went."

I noticed that she shot a deadly stare at Stanley. He must be involved also, swirled around in my thoughts. After all, it was him who introduced us to the Mozis in the first place.

"Mr. Mozi found himself in the middle of a major drug war. One of the lead figures was killed just two weeks ago, creating a fight for all of the power and control," she said, making a circle with her index finger.

Mom calmly sipped her _____ _____ ripping each other off and were exec_____ cash. It was open season as all sense o_____ was getting dangerous for Mozi and…"

"Rita, didn't I tell you not to give him _____ My stepfather interrupted. Mother glared at _____ spoke.

"Don't you tell me what to say to my son, p_____ snapped.

He let out a heavy huff and walked away. I he_____ mother's hand. It was clear she was angry with him and not n_____.

"Mom, what about Lolo?" I asked, thinking she was going to live with one of her many relatives.

Instead Mother hugged me and cried. Maybe my stepfather was also part of it all. What was his involvement? He was such a sissy-butt. Maybe he would be a lookout. I comforted her by gently patting her on the back. She smiled, looking me in the eyes. I could see her tears were still streaming.

"What I'm about to tell you son is going to be very…"

"Painful?" I asked.

She smiled, nodded her head. Mom cleared her throat before continuing.

...zi wanted to do what was right and went to the ... was going to be an informant and would have ... entire operation. "

...v did he plan on pulling this off? Witness protection?"

...other got quiet and all I could hear was the sound of ...th... k. It was the old-fashioned type with the bird singing ...ev...our. Mother had told me it was a gift from one of her ...uncl... His name was John. My mother kept his picture close to the lock along with a picture of her dad. Her father and uncle both had been police officers. My grandfather was killed in an automobile accident and his brother had been fatally shot.

"Men like Mr. Mozi most times outsmart themselves. He was in way too deep, and with his international scheme, there would never be anywhere on this planet to hide."

It was the police side of my mother I was listening to. All the training she had undergone made her hard at times. The police was here to serve and protect, she had told me. They will not bother you if you were doing the right thing.

Mr. Mozi had done the wrong thing and lost everything. Maybe his family would be deported back to Nigeria where they were from. Only Lolo was born here in America.

"Mom, can Lolo come and live with us?" I asked and did not expect the reaction I received.

My mother stared at me and let out a loud howl that brought my stepfather running back.

"Is everything all right?" he asked perplexed.

"Mom, what about Lolo? Could she come and live with us?" I repeated intentionally ignoring him.

He did not say anything. Stanley just glanced at me then at my mother.

"You still haven't told him what happened?" He asked, and for a moment mother said nothing. Then she slapped her leg and shouted.

"Didn't I ask you nicely not to disturb me? I'll deal with you later. Please excuse us."

She glanced at him and I've never seen Stanley move faster. I had to chuckle. He looked like a dog with his tail between his legs. No fight, I thought, and looked at mother again.

"Son, your mommy loves you and I wouldn't let anything happen to you."

I felt my heart slowly falling into my stomach. Then there was the sound of rumbling. I don't know if it was my stomach or the clock, or Stanley falling down the stairs.

"Shareef, Lolo, her mother, and her father were shot to death early this morning," my mother said.

Suddenly there was an eerie silence and everything seemed to stop. It was as if life ceased to exist. I could see myself running, but my feet did not move. I felt like I was trying to speak, but no sound came from my throat.

CHAPTER 3

I blinked twice trying to remember what had happened. Immediately my recollection overwhelmed me and I grabbed my mother in a tight embrace.

"Mom…" I cried and she held me.

"It's okay, Shareef," she said, hugging me. "I'm so sorry." It wasn't enough. A floodgate had opened and I couldn't stop crying. "How…? Why Lolo…?" I asked not wanting to believe.

"I don't know, sweetheart. It's crazy for you to understand, but I know Lolo had nothing to do with it."

My mom could see the pain on my face and paused. She wiped my forehead before continuing.

"Lolo was with her father and the bad guys he was working for, well, they somehow found out that he had been cooperating with the police investigations and they came after him. Lolo and her father were leaving for school. They were in his car when his former friends came. They fired thirty shots into the car. Some of the bullets hit Lolo and she was pronounced dead at the hospital," my mother said then she paused.

"But why kill Lolo? She's just a kid. She didn't do anything… She just wanted to help people and save the world."

"Those bastards were just ruthless. There was no real cause. They didn't give any of the family members a chance."

I heard her words and stared up at my mother in disbelief. She did not blink. There were no smiles just the cold facts. It was all too difficult for me to digest. My mother kept on speaking but I could no longer hear a word she was saying. I was in a fog somewhere else playing video games with Lolo.

We spent many hours playing her favorite game, *NBA Live*. I still have the last game we were playing saved. She liked playing only because I enjoyed playing it too, and she learned to play only because of me. We were like that from the day we met.

She was walking by my house wearing the same uniform that the girls wore at school. A quick calculation and I knew she was a student at my new school. Lolo was a very pretty and kind girl.

Meeting her was good because I had just transferred and knew no one at the school. Lolo and I became good friends right off the bat. Mother's story was a dagger through my heart.

"Mom please, say it's not true. Lolo is alive. She somehow made it out. She was…"

Mother was strong and never let me continue down the road of denial.

"I'm afraid she's gone. Sometimes only God can explain these mysteries. She was so young…" her voice trailed.

But I resisted accepting the reality. I needed to hear more.

"Son, there's no coming back from being shot dead. That's it," she said. Looking at the pity in her eyes made me want to scream. Mother held me. "Shareef," my mother cried. "It's for real. She was killed. I'm sorry…"

I heard my mother now and knew it was the truth. I realized Lolo would not come by talking about world peace anymore. I could not hold the feeling back, and I let out a blood-chilling scream from the depth of my stomach.

"No-o-o…!"

My mother could do nothing but hold me. She rocked back and forth just patting my back.

"It's okay, son. It's okay. She was my friend also," mother said, holding me in her arms. Together we cried for Lolo.

"No mom, say it's not true, please."

I can't remember how, but I must have fallen asleep in grief. I awoke later to find mother lying fast asleep next to me. I hugged her and closed my eyes. I watched as she got up and left me on the sofa. She went upstairs to her bedroom. I turned on the television and saw the news. I was overwhelmed by anxiety and hollered to my mother.

"Mom, mom, it's on the news! It's on the news!" I yelled.

She met me halfway up the stairs and we ran back down together. My stepfather slowly followed behind. We watched the whole story unfolding on the six o' clock news.

The report covered up how Mr. Mozi was killed and tagged it as a home invasion gone wrong. The news showed many of the foreign dignitaries who used to visit and who my family had met expressing their condolences. Something is not right. Their faces showed no remorse, but rather relief. They were all in it together. Something deep down inside told me they were scared for their own lives and who might be next. I glanced at my mother and stepdad, and saw that their eyes were riveted on the news report.

"Mom look, we met all those guys and their wives. Did you have any idea that they were doing all these bad things?"

"Ah, I wasn't aware per se..." she started and her voice trailed off.

Lolo's face appeared and the news hit home hard. I sat up, my mouth popped open and I stared blankly when the reporter confirmed what my mother had told me.

"...*The eleven-year-old daughter of Mr. and Mrs. Mozi, Lolo Mozi was rushed to the hospital and later pronounced dead.*"

A picture of a smiling Lolo and her father flashed momentarily across the TV. This was followed by a video of three bodies wrapped in body bags being carted away.

"...*It happened this morning at about seven o'clock as Mr. Mozi readied to take his daughter to school. Gunmen waiting outside his home greeted his Mercedes with gunshots from all angles. The would-be robbers fled the scene leaving all the valuables behind. The investigation is ongoing and the police are predicting an arrest will be made in the next several days. This is Andy Redding reporting for Channel 4 News.*"

"I can't watch this anymore."

I got up and searched for the remote but it was nowhere in sight. I ran up the stairs to my room and threw myself on the bed. I must have passed out because when I awoke both my mother and stepfather were standing over me anxiously. I blinked hard to regain consciousness.

"Are you feeling better, Shareef? I was about to call the doctor," my mother said. I felt groggy, but I knew I did not need a doctor or hospital. Not now. I needed to be close to home.

"I feel okay…" I started when my stepfather interrupted.

"Maybe a little soup will make him feel better," he suggested.

I hated soup, but said nothing when I saw my mother nodding in agreement. She stared at me for a minute then said, "Yes, please go and get him some. I'll sit with him." When my stepfather abruptly walked out the room, my mother shouted, "Thanks!"

I closed my eyes as I heard his footsteps going down the stairs. My mother rubbed my forehead and said, "He carried you upstairs right after you passed out. Are you feeling better? I think I should call Doctor Grant anyway."

"No mom, really I feel alright. I just blanked out… All

that news and stuff about Lolo and her family sent me."

"I know, son, it's a lot of sad information coming at once. I know you're overwhelmed by it all. But please try to understand and don't let this incident cloud your outlook on life."

"Yes mother."

"Have you eaten? I don't think you've eaten anything since school and it's almost eight. I'll go fix your favorite frozen pizza. How about that…?"

"That's fine, mother," I said, mustering a smile.

She kissed my forehead and smiled at me before leaving the room. The door had barely closed when all of a sudden I felt really alone. I wanted to call her back, but I hesitated.

"You've gotta learn how to be a man…"

That was what my real father always told me. He would tell me that every time my mother left me with him and I'd cry for her. I remember staring back at him not understanding.

I understood today. Lolo was gone. I stared at the game station and felt a sickness rising in my stomach. I could not go to it right now. It felt like I was disrespecting her or something. Lolo was a good friend. The thought made my tears fall on the pillow. I wiped my eyes and sat up in the bed, but the heavy thoughts still weighed me down.

CHAPTER 4

The funeral seemed to arrive quickly. It took the Mozi family and their friends one week to plan. The morning of the funeral was surreal. Three closed caskets, camera crews, police, diplomatic plates everywhere, stretch limos, expensive foreign cars, and people dressed in all black. I stood frozen watching them lower the caskets into the grave plots. I threw eleven long-stemmed roses into the dirt for my best friend Lolo. The rest of the funeral was a haze, and ended with me in a dark cloud.

The drive home was silent. I went straight to my room

without a word to anyone. I could not help but hear the shouting. I strained to hear what the fuss was between my mother and stepfather.

"I don't care that you're a schoolteacher! You will go down to the precinct tomorrow and talk to the detective who has been calling all day. I don't think…"

"Why do I have to be the one who is always doing as you say, Rita?" Before mother could answer, he continued. "It's the same thing you told Mozi, and you see what that got him. Both he and his whole family are lying in the morgue, filled with bullet holes…"

"They were casualties of a drug war that you're going to sit idly by and watch spin out of control," she answered acidly.

"Yeah. That's how the police look at what I was doing? Or is that how they deal with the drug war?" He spat the words with scorn.

"Don't start with me…" mother warned.

"Aw c'mon Rita, give me a break. The police did not care what the cost was. All they seemed to want to do is arrest the…"

"You're telling me you would rather support these drug dealers and…"

"I'm not saying that I'm supporting anyone. This is my life you're talking about. Did you see what happened to Mozi? And he was one of theirs."

"You are scared to cooperate with the investigation, aren't you?"

"Scared? What are you talking about? I have worked in the public school system for the past ten years with some of the scariest kids this side of the world, and you have the nerve to call me scared."

"Then explain not wanting to cooperate with the police and…"

"I don't want to be killed—that's the reason. It's that simple. Hate me because I'd rather live. But let me tell you, those guys… Whoever killed Mozi and Lolo were good at what they do."

"Maybe it's more than just that, huh?"

I sat on the stairs and waited for his answer. He must have given the wrong one. Mother was definitely heated. She stomped out of the kitchen and threw herself against the sofa. She settled when she saw me looking.

"Shareef, are you hungry, baby?" she asked, and I nodded. She walked to the bottom of the stairs. "Go back and lay down, love, I will bring you something to eat, okay?"

Although she was being super-cautious with me, I could tell that she was holding back her anger. I was relieved that she was not mad at me. I made my way inside the room and turned the television on. I laid down not really looking at the television thinking about why my mother seemed so angry.

Was it because Stanley was in some way blaming her for Mr. Mozi's and Lolo's death? I wonder how much my parents knew about all this mess with the Mozis, and why was she pressuring Stanley to go to the police? Regardless, she must have used her motherly radar on me because she walked in carrying a tray of my favorite food. She wore that nice motherly compassionate look she had when reporters were on television interviewing her after she arrested that boy she said reminded her of me.

"Mom, why are you and Stanley arguing?" I asked and watched her set the tray in front of me. She pushed the glass of milk toward me.

"Here, get something in your stomach before you start worrying too much about grown folks' business."

I sipped the milk and munched on a few cookies before I asked again.

"You know all evening you've been acting strange. I know Lolo's death has something to do with it, but there seems to be more going on."

"What's this? Too much *Law and Order.* I swear I'm going to monitor how much you watch these programs on TV. They makes you kids think you know more than you do," she said. I could see this was going to be tough.

I munched on more cookies. Somewhere between watching me sip milk and furtive glances at the television, mother began to speak. I sat up and paid close attention.

"Son, whenever you know something about a crime or something bad that has happened, please come and share it with me."

She held my shoulders as she spoke.

"Yes mom."

"I'm your mother and I know what's right for you. If I tell you that the matter should be discussed with the police, then I think that's the best thing for you to do. Trust me," she said in her sincerest of tones.

"Yes mommy," I said, nodding.

"Your stepfather does not feel it's right that I should tell him to cooperate with the police and that's what you overheard.

We were discussing the pros and cons of talking to the police, that's all, Shareef."

My stepfather walked in as if on cue.

"I've got cheese puffs and 7UP," he announced. Mother and I shot him a dirty look.

"Didn't I tell you not to give him junk?"

"But I thought-"

"Stanley, let me tell you a few things," mother said. Her voice warned that she was not feeling him. "First of all, Shareef was hungry and I gave him something to snack on. Secondly he's my son and if I want to give him a snack then I can."

"You call milk and cookies healthy?"

"Look, I'm really not going to sit here and argue about this. You can take this tray and your greasy chips downstairs when you go. Thank you," mother said.

Her tone left no doubt that there was a war brewing between them. My stepfather handily grabbed the tray with the cookies and milk.

"I'll see you downstairs," he said. I made a face as he went out the door.

"I don't want any of..."

"Shareef, don't start with me. Please have some. Stanley

brought it for you," she said, throwing me a deadly glance.

Then my mother walked out and closing the door behind her. I waited until I heard her muffled footsteps fading then I put down the snack and tiptoed to the door. Slowly, I opened it. My guess was that they would continue to argue and I wanted to know what all the fuss was really about. I peeked out at the landing and heard anger in their voices.

"How many times do I have to tell you not to argue with me in front of Shareef? I told you it's not a nice thing for him to experience. I want the best for my child, and I certainly don't need someone who's constantly trying to embarrass me."

"Look, I'm wrong, but…"

"But nothing! Always with the excuses…! But this and but that… Just don't let it happen again. That's really all there is to it."

"You're right…"

"You're goddamn right, I'm right. And I'm right about you going tomorrow downtown and meet with the detectives. You really do need to come clean with your story."

"What do you mean come clean? I've told them all I know."

"No you haven't." I had to run to bed and sneeze before

returning and checking if either of them detected that I was listening. In other households, eavesdropping may not be a serious offense but around these parts it carried consequences. Needless to say I was really cautious.

"You're always speculating. I can see why your relationships failed. You're suspicious of everyone."

"Do not throw my past in my face. You have no right to rehash my past because I shared something with you. You're not perfect either. Your wife divorced you, didn't she?"

"So? We needed to be through with that lie we were living."

"Well, if you don't go and tell them everything you know, and I do mean everything, we are going to be through with this lie."

"You call this a lie? I've been real with you."

"I'm in law enforcement."

"I know. So…?"

"Then you should know that I know everything that happened with you and the Mozis."

"Yeah, you should. We went to several of their parties."

"That is true. But I never went on the out-of-town trips."

"That's because of those awful hours you work."

"Alright, but I never went to the Las Vegas and the trips to the Bahamas and Mexico, Brazil, Jamaica. Should I continue?"

My mother probably knew much more but liked to tease you into thinking she did not. It was her way of leveling the playing field. My stepfather stood up and began retracing that groove in the floor he had made earlier while pacing. After going back and forth, he paused and answered.

"I didn't do anything wrong," he said then continued pacing.

"I never said that you did," my mother replied.

"You sound like there was something else going on besides someone inviting me on a trip."

"You went on several trips."

"Yeah, but I never did anything wrong."

"If you did, would you tell me?"

"Of course I…"

"Then why don't you be honest now and 'fess up to all…"

"You're trying to incriminate me. I…"

"You can plead the Fifth, but remember the police—we have our ways of finding things out."

"That's what this is about, huh? Are you trying to find

out something to—to tell your friends?"

"You underestimate us. Those detectives have already pinpointed you in lots of those parties in Vegas. Back in early January, a waitress was murdered. She was last seen at one of the parties you attended. She spent the night in your room. Need I say more?"

Her words stopped him in his tracks and he looked like he had been hit with a low hard blow that ripped his breath away. My stepfather seemed to be reeling when he looked up and our eyes collided.

"Shareef, what're doing?" he asked, startling me.

"Uh, nothing, just coming to get a drink of water."

"Shareef, were you eavesdropping again? You better not be, Mister. Get in your bed right now!" Mother angrily shouted.

I closed the door quickly and made a running leap into the bed. There were no further stirrings heard. I waited for the inevitable to happen. Mother would soon come barging into my room to read the sentencing. This time there would be no need for a trial; I was caught red-handed.

How could I reverse this situation? She shouldn't be mad at me, I thought. Thinking quickly I grabbed my backpack and pulled out the textbook for tonight's homework. By the time they made it up the stairs I was already in the throes of doing homework. Mother peeked in.

"Shareef, don't worry about your homework. I will contact the school and tell them you will make up the work this weekend," she said then closed the door.

I smiled. Lolo and I always did this. Anytime you get in trouble reach for the schoolbook, sit at the desk and act like you're stressing the work. It works. But the idea made me drift back to thinking about Lolo and her father. I had a lot of questions to ask my mother, but now was not a good time.

CHAPTER 5

I was at the desk staring at the pages in front of me. Tears were rolling and my thoughts were going crazy as I remembered my friend and felt the heartbreak. Lolo was a good person. She did not sell drugs or kill anyone. She was a victim of her parents' circumstances and actions. It made no sense to me.

I couldn't shake the feeling that mom and Stanley were hiding something from me. I wished my mother was in the mood to talk, but she had not attempted to discuss her or Stanley's involvement. It seemed crazy that my mother could be involved in the death of my friend. I wanted desperately to know what was going on.

My thoughts were interrupted by the sound of the knob twisting and the clanging sound of my mother's silver charm bracelet.

"Shareef, I know you are going through a lot right now, but can we need talk about what happened in school today?" I was not ready with all my questions, but I tried to get her to talk.

"Are you still angry about what happened at school?"

"Shareef, I've spoken to your principal and I thought you did nothing wrong. I'm not going to be angry with you for standing up for yourself. You're growing, and you're going to have your own independent feelings about everything. I just hope you learn to look at things rationally and be respectful at all times. Okay?"

"Mom, are you okay? I mean you're not mad, right?"

"No Shareef. I'm not mad at you, son."

"Then can I ask, why are you angry at Stanley?"

"Oh please," she sighed, sounding exasperated. "He and I do not see eye to eye on all things. That's it. You can stop interrogating me about grown folks' business."

"Mom, I'm gonna miss Lolo." I heard myself saying it,

but really didn't know where that came from.

"I love you, son," she said, and I could feel her tears on my cheek when she drew me close.

"I love you."

We stayed that way for a good minute until mother regained her composure. She walked away, picking up my clothes. Then she turned back to me.

"Okay Shareef, you're going to have to do a better job of keeping your room clean. We gave the maid the year off so please cooperate. Go get cleaned up and ready for bed."

With that, she swept out the door, and I heard her footsteps running downstairs. I slowly got up and stared at the Lebron James poster on the wall above my bed. Then I got ready to go to sleep. This was absolutely the worst day I'd ever had. I kept thinking about my good friend, Lolo, and how she died.

It slowly dawned on me that there would be no making up with Lolo. There was no way she could come back from death. I felt a sadness brewing in me, and closed my eyes to contain it but the tears came anyway. The door opened and mother walked into my room. Bending forward, she planted a goodnight kiss on my forehead.

"Shareef, you will be a better person for this," she said

softly. I stared at her with questions reeling in my head. I wasn't able to immediately understand her, and was still thinking about being a better person when I heard her say, "Please try to get some sleep, Shareef," she smiled that motherly smile. Then she kissed me again, and hugged me. Walking away from my bed, she asked, "Do you want the light off?"

It was the same question she had asked when she arrested that boy who was my age. I nodded not because I was scared, I just didn't want to see the shadows.

"Good night, son."

"Good night, mom."

I closed my eyes but could not stop thinking. She was a good person. Even though she was scared of insects, Lolo hated to see even them dying.

"Help him, Shareef," she used to shout whenever we would come across an insect in need.

Lolo was the best friend I ever had and I could feel my thoughts roaming out of control. Then the realization of the loss hit me. And as hard as I tried, I just couldn't prevent my tears from streaming down. The night wore on and I realized how quiet it was. Slowly I went to the window where I sat listening to the nocturnal sounds. After a while I realized that birds were whistling. It was daylight.

The sad moon, even though fading, was still staring down. It was goodbye to a yesterday that I'll never forget, but it was a new day. I've got to find out what's going on. I heard faint sounds of chatter and I inched closer to mother's bedroom. I could hear them arguing. Stanley sounded really angry. My ears strained to listen.

"I don't give a rat's tail what the detectives told you, Rita. I was not having sex with dancers in Vegas. I went to the party, then left and went back to the hotel alone."

Mother and Stanley were still arguing. I continued listening as Stanley spoke.

"Mozi and his buddies went in another room to have a nightcap. From that point, I was asleep. I told you the plane ride was long, and I wasn't feeling well."

"It just so happens that condoms were found in your room…"

"Hey, those could've been there before I got there."

"I suppose the whole janitorial staff cannot see, huh Stanley?"

"No, I'm not saying that. I'm saying that I know nothing of that girl's death. Nothing…"

"Stanley, there are eyewitnesses who saw you and Mozi with her. They were staying in the same hotel as you and Mozi. Don't lie to me, Stanley. I know you very well!"

"I swear to you, Rita. I've never met that woman until we were all in the club. I don't care what your police friends shared with you, I know that I had nothing to do with her death."

There was a long pause and I felt like I wanted to sneeze but this was too interesting to leave. I wanted to learn more. It was obvious that Lolo and her father were not the only ones who had been killed in connection with this drug gang. I waited holding my nose to prevent the sneeze from coming out. I had to know why mother and Stanley were up arguing about Lolo's parents.

Something in what he said made my mother's voice of authority relax. "I'll level with you; Detective Johnson thinks you know way more than you are volunteering. That's why he wants you to come down to the precinct."

"Well level with me some more. Do I need an attorney or not?"

"Are you being honest with me? I don't know—I can't tell anymore. And that's the real deal. I mean if I'm wrong, then God forgive me, but I don't know about you…"

"You know me. You've seen my family. You know both my children, and I've never hidden anything from you. Am I anything like what you're thinking? My cheating wife is the reason I am divorced. Just because Mozi was a front man for a drug cartel doesn't mean I cheated on you."

"I don't know. I just want you to go downtown and clear this situation up."

"Will that make you feel better? If it's going to make you feel any better then I'll go down tomorrow and take the damn lie detector test they have been asking me to take. Then you can get off my back."

"I'll be happy when you clear it all up."

"You think that's going to be the end of it? They're going to want more and more."

"If you're not implicated in any of the wrongdoing, then we'll be alright. If you fail the test, then you'll need a good criminal attorney."

"What about the bad guys? Think they'll be happy that I'm going to the police?"

"Don't worry about that."

"Are you crazy? Didn't you see what happened to Mozi? The moment he went to the police. Pow! His family... You wanna live with that, Rita?"

"Easy, Mister," my mother said, her tone laced with resentment. "First of all I did not pull the trigger. Secondly I wasn't there, telling Mozi to launder money taken off drug dealing, robbery or extortion, okay? I advised him to talk with the lead detectives because they saw something on film involving you."

"I know everything will be alright. I did nothing wrong. All I did was travel to Vegas, and the Bahamas with a friend who turned out to be involved with…"

"The truth is you took gifts of trips with known felons. You didn't know their true identities, but you willingly cooperated with them and may have been a mule or a keeper of drugs. Now you must cooperate with law enforcement or your freedom will be curtailed. It is that simple, Stanley."

I had heard enough and walked away from my listening position near the door. I slipped back into my room unnoticed and restless. My mind was racing, and my thoughts kept swirling around Lolo. Glancing at the clock, it was going on three in the morning. I tried closing my eyes, but kept seeing Lolo in my memories. I knew I wouldn't be able to get any sleep. I kept thinking that I just have to get out of here. I've got to see for myself what happened.

I rose to my feet, threw on my gear, and grabbed my spare key. I've never been much for sneaking out, but something just came over me. As I tiptoed out of my bedroom I was terrified that someone would suddenly feel like using the bathroom. My heart was pounding. My mom would be furious if she knew what I was doing. And Stanley was already a snitch, but more so with my mom's missiles pointed at him. He just couldn't wait to aim them right at me, the easy target. The carpeting muffled my footsteps, so I easily slipped out my room. Tiptoeing, I made it past their bedroom, and was in the clear. I walked down the stairs slowly and headed for the kitchen. I closed my eyes and took a deep breath. I knew that once I turned the knob, there was no way out of trouble if I were to get caught.

ANTHONY WHYTE

CHAPTER 6

I did it. I was able to make it out of the house. This part
of the neighborhood was nothing like the busy street I lived on.
Here no one was awake, there was no corner store, no one out
sipping booze out of bottles covered with brown paper bags.
Out here it was just the squirrels, the cold early morn, and I. My
feet moved swiftly as I did not want to be out for too long or too
late. I walked as close to the edge of the sidewalks to keep the
motion lights from the dark homes from turning on and catching
me out at this late hour of the night. The whole neighborhood is

sleeping, not a light on or a sound.

My heart sank as I saw the yellow tape. Never before had this community been decorated with such a display. I wanted to turn back around, and run home. I felt dizzier with each step I took closer to the scene the crime. I slipped around back where Lolo once told me they kept a spare key under a fake rock. As I held it in my hand, I almost wanted there to be no key so I would have a good excuse to turn around and slip back into my bed. I turned the fake rock over, and there it was—a silver key.

Removing the key from its hiding place, I slid it inside the keyhole. Then I entered the kitchen by turning the key. It was eerie to be in someone's home like this. There was still coffee sitting on the counter, a newspaper laying across the table, dishes in the sink, and one of the cabinets half open. The house felt abandoned, as if the family had suddenly up and moved did not even have time to tidy up or pack. I could hear no sounds other than my breath and heartbeat. I moved from the kitchen into the living room, and could see the bloodstains on the floor. I moved quickly past it to avoid getting caught in the horrific drama, and emotion of the sight.

I pushed myself up the stairs and crept into Lolo's room.

It felt so cold without Lolo. I felt obligated to be here but at the same time I felt like an intruder. I walked over to the computer, which was still on, and held a draft of her latest save-the-world plans. The place was tidy. Nothing was out of place. I found her book of her poetry. One of her many aspirations was to be an author. Her words had always been much more articulate than mine. She managed to make her poetry sound like 'the new Black', while mine sounded like a dead language.

Sitting on her bed, I carefully thumbed through the pages. Suddenly I heard movement and sprang into action. Quickly turning off the light, I shoved the poetry book into my pocket. Then I slid under her bed, knowing that whoever was in the house with me expected no one would be here.

I could hear the faint sounds of more than one person moving, and then more loudly I heard footsteps above me, below me, and moving down the halls. My heart raced louder and faster. I heard someone standing by the door.

He pushed the door open and was about to search the room when a voice said, "Where is it? Where is the key to the safe?" The steps of the strange figure could be heard moving further away. Just then, the voice of another man said, "He kept the key in the desk. Top drawer. There is a hidden compartment.

Just feel around for it."

That voice sounded familiar but I could not make it out because they were whispering. I heard nothing further. How am I going to slip out of here? I thought. I crawled from under the bed on my stomach and peeked out through the open door. I searched the hallway as far as my eyes could see and saw only shadowy figures in the study. This might be my only chance to get out. I stayed low and used the darkness to shield me from their sight. I heard the familiar voice once again.

"I cannot go down for this! I have to get out of here before someone notices I am missing."

Another voice replied, "What do you mean *you* cannot go down for this? You already know what the deal is. Don't even think about snitching, if you know what's good for you!"

"I would never dare speak. You know me. You know that I'm not like that. I would never dare betray you," the familiar voice squeaked.

"You see what happens to snitches! Go! Get your punk ass out of here. As of right now, your usefulness has reached its limit."

I heard footsteps drawing near. I slithered into Mr. and Mrs. Mozi's bedroom. I had never seen this room before. It was the perfect hiding place because I could hear everything happening in the next room and would know when the bad guys made their exit.

"Would you look at this? This man was about to bury us," a voice said.

I heard the footsteps moving quickly down the stairs and out the door. Who was that voice? Who could it be? My mind was swirling, my heart racing, and I was trapped.

When I was certain I was alone in the house, I decided to look around for anything they missed. I turned on the light in the Mozi bedroom to see if Mr. Mozi had anything hidden in here.

Once the lights were on, a beautiful matching bedroom set was revealed with only one piece that did not match. It was an old secretary desk. I opened it and discovered stacks of pictures taken on a yacht. The men were all holding their left hands up in the pictures. They were sporting matching pinky rings with black jade and garnet. Stanley was in all of these pictures. He had the same ring as the men he was pictured with.

I had noticed both Stanley and Mr. Mozi had these rings, but had just thought they shared the same poor taste in gaudy jewelry. Mr. Mozi's ring was also in the desk. I pocketed the pictures and the ring. Mom was right. Stanley was more involved than he let on.

While searching the desk drawers, I stumbled upon a gold chain, and hanging from it a gold skeleton key. I remember Lolo used to wear this around her neck whenever Mr. Mozi's business partners came to town. I took the key, put it around my neck. This key must be to something, and there must have been a reason Lolo wore it at those moments.

The sun was starting to rise. How long had I been here? I had to get home before I was missed. I raced down the stairs, and out the back door. I cut through the neighbors' backyards to avoid being seen by those starting their early-morning commute. I was lucky. No one spotted me slipping in the backdoor of our home. Once safe inside, I put all the things I found inside my backpack.

I threw on my pajamas, and jumped in my bed. Then I closed my eyes, trying to catch some sleep before mother's wake-up call.

CHAPTER 7

The sun came up too early that morning. It was Friday, and I pushed myself slowly out of bed after hearing my mother yelling.

"Shareef, come on let's go. You've got school, young man."

She darted in and out of my room at rapid pace. Rolling over, I sought the comfort of my pillow and covers, but I would not rest for long. Her flurry of movements continued to disturb the sleep coming over me.

She would take me to school as soon as I was ready but she was not going to allow me to be late. No way.

"Shareef, I know you don't think you're going to just lay around and be late for school?"

"No mom, I'm up…" I yawned.

"C'mon Shareef, get in the bathroom now."

There was a strong sense of urgency in my mother's voice. I quickly jumped out of my comfortable bed then ran to the bathroom. Later at breakfast she explained that my father would come and get me from school.

"Where are you going to be, mom?"

"I'll be in an important meeting with your stepfather," she answered.

"Your meeting is too important for you to come and get me yourself?" I asked in my most pitiful tone. I hated when she took time out for Stanley at my expense.

"Shareef, please do not start. This is a very, very important meeting, okay? So please just this once, okay? I will make it up to you."

"Okay mom," I said gratefully. "Why can't grandma pick me up, mom?" I asked trying to push for an advantage. If grandma picked me up, I would be able to eat whatever I wanted and there would be a good surprise.

My grandmother seemed to always have a neat gift stashed away waiting for me to come by and claim it. My mother was wagging her index finger indicating that grandma was out of the question.

"But why?" I insisted.

"Shareef, sweetheart, grandma has a medical appointment and will not be able to."

"Grandma is sick?"

"Not really, she had a medical appointment prior to all this and it is too much of an emergency for her, okay?"

"Okay," I sighed, disappointed.

"Now your father will get you after school and I will pick you up from his place, okay, Shareef?"

"It's his girlfriend's place," my mother sort of giggled before she answered.

"Go brush your hair," she answered.

Maybe I wasn't moving fast enough because before I could walk away and honor her request, she was repeating her directive.

"Shareef, didn't I tell you to brush your hair?" she said.

Turning back, I raced upstairs back to my room. I did a dance while I brushed my hair. Then I raced downstairs feeling better than I did when I awoke.

"I'm ready," I announced. My mother gave me the once-over. She hand-brushed my hair before she nodded her approval.

"Okay your father will pick you up after school," she repeated.

"I know, mom. "

"And don't give him any trouble," my mother warned.

I could feel every syllable. After that my head felt like mush. I was tired and almost fell asleep over the cereal. I wanted to see what was going on between my mother and Stanley so I managed to stay awake.

They tried to keep it normal asking each other to pass the toast in friendly voices, but I sensed they were seething under the cordiality. Mother and my stepfather ate mostly in silence. I guessed they did not want me to hear any of the 'adult' stuff.

Stanley seemed agitated drinking his coffee and staring off into space like he was a kid caught playing a foolish prank. In the midst of our silence, the cup rattled loudly against the saucer as he set it down. He offered a frown. I smiled.

"C'mon Shareef, we don't have all day. I have to go with

Stanley to the precinct and then to our meeting—"

"You don't have to go anywhere with me. It is your choice to go," Stanley said.

"Okay," she said, staring at him before continuing. "Because I have chosen to attend an important meeting with Stanley."

"Do you have to tell this eleven-year-old everything? I mean what don't you tell him?"

"I try to be as honest with my son and I expect everyone around me to be the same way. C'mon Shareef, let's put a rush on this breakfast," mother said and my stepfather left the breakfast table. "Shareef, we can't be late."

She was always rushing in the morning. I heard Stanley's voice grumbling in the background.

"You better do as your mother says and stop falling asleep."

It sounded like the voice of a disgruntled man. I guessed he returned to try and put some of the spotlight on me. I yawned and nodded then left out the door. All three of us got in the car. My stepfather appeared flustered and nervous as the car pulled out of the garage. He was dressed in his best blue suit, white shirt and red tie. Mom was outfitted in a gray suit and white blouse.

She carried a black handbag. I've seen my mother dressed like this once before. She was going to a court. It was a custody battle for me.

That day, my father showed up to court wearing dirty, blue jeans, and there was alcohol on his breath. It wasn't a fair fight. The judge readily awarded custody to my mother. I would get to see my father whenever my mother allowed. Like that day, today she was on a mission, but did not want to discuss what it was.

She was my mother and I ignored all the warning signs. Maybe Stanley wanted to be nice and talk about the itinerary. I tried to engage him.

"You're not going to work today?" I asked, looking at him.

He looked at me as if he wanted to open up and talk, but could not speak at this time. I understood. Maybe he was on punishment. The idea brought a smile to my face.

"All right, everyone's in? Let's go," mother said in an authoritative tone as she glanced back.

The car was in reverse, and this brought back vivid memories of Lolo. Again she would not be in school today or any day after. I felt emptiness building in the pit of my gut. This feeling combined with my lack of sleep inspired me to want to skip school.

Today I didn't, I wanted to attend because of Lolo. School was probably a refuge for her. Too bad she couldn't live there. She would probably still be alive today.

"Buckle your seatbelt, please."

My mother's words brought me back to the bright light of reality. The sun shone and I saw birds flying around in the early morning dew. Life had moved on. The car was traveling and I really did not want to go, but I was going anyway. I miss you Lolo, I whispered as we drove by where she had spent the last seconds of her life.

My anger spread with each breath. I sat in the back listening to the radio and staring at nothing. The world has suffered a loss, I thought as we turned on to the main street. A traffic accident slowed traffic down.

Mother tapped her fingers on the steering wheel and while my stepfather stared straight ahead. Watching him squirming around in his seat, I noticed his trembling fingers and how he kept fixing his collar. Seeing him that nervous was the best part of the day and I almost laughed out loud. I yawned disturbing the silence, then the next I knew, I awoke to find my mother's eyes glued on me.

"Did you get any sleep whatsoever, Shareef? I don't think you did," mother said, monitoring me from the rearview.

I tried to stay awake, but that was not happening. The comfortable leather of the car along with snug fit of my headset made it easy for me to set off on my own voyage. I was walking side by side with Lolo again. She was talking about solving world hunger. I was trying not to hear her until she began to float away like a cloud. She was above me warning me to take her a little more seriously.

"Shareef, Shareef, you better get moving…"

"Yes, I don't know where to start, Lolo…"

"Shareef honey, are you sleeping? You were dreaming."

I stared wide-eyed at my mother and made every effort to get out of the fog out my brain. I shook my head and wiped my eyes waiting for the confusion to clear. Lolo seemed so real but it was all a dream. My mother waited on me while my stepfather watched uninterested, still wearing a frown.

"Are we there yet, mom?" I asked, and her nod seemed restrained. It was as if she was not trying to let me go inside the school.

"Do you feel better, Shareef?" mother asked.

The question lingered for a while. I was busy trying to decide if I wanted to lie so I would not have to go to school. I remembered seeing Lolo's face and hearing her voice.

"Maybe the whole thing is overwhelming to Shareef. Look at his face, he seems to be confused," Stanley said.

"You could be right, Stanley. I think I'll go tell his teacher," mother said before getting out the car.

"I feel alright. I was just dreaming that's all," I answered.

I wanted to go to school because I wanted to check out Lolo's locker. There might be some more clues as to who killed her and her family. She used to keep a photo journal of all of the diplomats and important dudes who came around. I got out of the car, kissed my mother and waved at Stanley. Before she returned to the car my mother asked again.

"Shareef, are you sure?" she said.

"I'll be alright, mom. I'll see you later," I smiled and walked away with bravery written on my face.

"Remember, Lenny will come by later and get you here. Do not give him any problems, please. Shareef, give mommy a hug and I'll see you later," she said as we embraced again and again. My mother seemed a little on the edge the way she was hugging me. We both smiled, she waved and I walked away.

I felt her eyes following me as I set off across the schoolyard feeling a little stupid. Today I was given the ultimate test. Maybe she wanted to see if I would not want to attend. But I wanted to be in school mostly because I knew that was the way Lolo would have wanted it. Because of my fallen friend I found the strength to go past the excuses and go to school. My determination to get to the bottom of what happened to Lolo and how my mom and Stanley may have been involved was overwhelming. I turned and waved at my mother still watching me, then walked through the doors.

Before the morning break, I was able to slip down the hall to Lolo's locker. She gave me the combo in case I forgot one of my textbooks at home. When I opened it, I could not help but notice that everything looked neat and untouched. Her locker, much like her room, was a well-oiled machine of efficiency. I swiped a picture book, which had images of the United Nations, the White House, and the Washington Monument on its cover. If only she knew what her father was up to. She had to know. Lolo was way too smart not to have figured it out. I noticed a photo that she and I had taken together when we went to the museum. She had drawn a heart around us and written *'Lolo and Shareef'*. I could feel a tear gathering at my pupil. I carefully tucked the photograph away in a secret compartment in my backpack where it could not be crushed. I sped to homeroom so that no one would notice my detour.

Once I got there, the wicked witch of the sixth grade was waiting. Miss Brown rode her broom to the front of the room.

"Some of us may already know of the unfortunate circumstances surrounding the death of one of ours," Miss Brown started.

She seemed to stab at her cracking, caked makeup. I felt like crying too but I knew the others were watching and waiting for me to break down. After what happened in the lunchroom yesterday, I did not want to give them that satisfaction. I pursed my lips and listened. I could hear the rumblings of those who had not been watching their television.

"Who's she talking about?" a classmate wondered aloud.

"Must be one of the teachers, I hope it's mine."

"You must not have done your homework again."

"Maybe we'll get a cute teacher…"

"I don't know."

"Why don't you just shut up and listen. I'm trying to hear what is being said," I said louder than I intended. I never realized that I had disturbed everyone until I saw that all eyes were on me. My apparent outburst gave the witch a chance to swoop down on me.

"Shareef, would you mind showing a little reverence? We are very saddened by the death of one your classmates, and you're over there disrespectfully running your mouth."

She was trying to put an evil spell on me. I knew I was not the one who was showing disrespect.

"Miss Brown…" I started, but before I could defend myself, she started yelling.

"I will discuss this matter with you after the morning's assembly," she barked. It was embarrassing and I was not the cause for the disruption. The witch continued with her incantations. "Any more problems from you and you will be in the principal's office, young man," she said, giving me a mean stare.

I held my head up, returning her stare. I did not want to back down anymore.

"Lolo Mozi was killed in an unfortunate incident which also took her parents' lives. We at the school are reaching out to the relatives of Lolo. Please keep her and her family in your prayers. If any of you was close to her, please come and see me at the guidance office."

I felt her breathing on me and knew the witch was in my face.

"Young man, I want to see you in my office, now!" She ordered.

I was a little peeved, but I followed her directions without protest and moved out.

CHAPTER 8

I sat outside Miss Brown's office waiting for her and wishing that I never attended this school. I imagined Miss Brown riding her broomstick around the hallways harassing stragglers who were late for class. Then miraculously she appeared, walked past me and motioned for me to follow her. I did as requested. I walked into her lair regretting that I came to school today.

"Shareef, I don't know what is the matter with you, but you're asking to be punished. Now, I don't want to hear another peep out of you for the rest of the day. Are you listening to me?"

"Yes Miss Brown," I said obediently. I could not

understand why she was so ready to have a fight with me. "I was not trying to disrespect anybody, and especially not Lolo."

"Be on your best behavior because you're very close to drawing a suspension," she said and I nodded. "Now go and join your class," she said, writing a note, and handing it to me. "Give this to the teacher."

"Okay," I said then hastened out her office.

Stress was holding me captive, and a feeling of discomfort dogged me. As I walked slowly clutching the note in my hand, I could only remember Lolo. I am wasting time in school when I could be investigating.

My early morning excursion to Lolo's was somewhat like a dream. Those guys were looking for something. I needed to know what was going on. I realized in that instant that the teacher would not notice I had not returned. The teacher might actually assume that I was going to be out for the day.

I dodged people's notice and tucked into the boys' room. How was I going to pull this off? I had never cut school before. The kids at my old public school used to do it all the time. They told me that the trick was leaving through the cafeteria doors. The only staff down there are in the kitchen and don't notice a kid or the sound of a door closing. And the one benefit of private school is no hall monitors. All teachers are in their classrooms and anyone else is in the teacher's lounge or their office. My heart was racing.

After taking one deep breath, I pushed the doors of the bathroom open. The halls were deserted. I walked slowly down the hall, and ducked low as to not be seen through the glass windows of the classroom doors. Once I made it to the stairway, I was more than half way there. I peeked into the cafeteria. The principal was down there with the maintenance staff. I ducked back quickly. I had to think fast. The chapel.

The morning mass was always open to the public and the doors would be unlocked. Mass wasn't scheduled for a couple hours. This was my only chance. I walked quickly to the chapel, and as expected, there was no one in sight. I pushed the doors open and instantly felt the morning air hit my face. Victory. If I get caught, my mom would definitely put me under the jail.

Once out, I moved quickly catching the first bus to head home. I decided I needed some insurance in case this plan fell apart. Mom was with Stanley, and grandma was at an appointment. The only one left is my dad. Dad told me about all the stunts he used to pull when he was my age. At least if I had him on my side, I could get some mercy. I pulled out my phone to call him.

"Hello. Shareef? You out of school already?"

"Hey dad. I left school early. I was feeling really sick," I said in my most pathetic sounding voice.

"Your mom told me that you weren't yourself. Do you still need me to come pick you up?"

"No. I just need you to call mom and tell her I left early. I tried calling her but she did not answer."

"Your mother does not know you left school early? How did you leave?"

"I just left. I could not stand being there anymore. All I can think about is Lolo," I said, hoping that he would understand.

"I can't believe you! Okay, I am going to call the school and tell them that I came by to get you early since you were feeling sick. But I am coming to get you! You are not going home to just have fun playing video games. You will be here with me, and I will be putting you to work. Right now I am at a new site and can't leave early. I can't pick you up until three-o'clock. You had better be at the door and ready to go. Do you hear me young man?"

"Yes dad," I said.

The call ended and I could breathe a sigh of relief. Had

this been mom, she would have ordered me to go right back to school. I have until 3'oclock to look around and at least this time, there would be daylight. I just wished I knew what I was looking for.

The bus was empty at this time of the morning. The ride felt so long. I pulled out the picture that Lolo had kept of us. All this time, I did not notice she had a crush on me. I liked her too. Why did she not say anything? I was too busy thinking about things that don't really matter, like NBA players and video games.

I felt the tears gather in my eyes, hitting the photo in my hand. I closed my eyes and let the memories hit me. She was my first love. I loved Lolo and now, I would never have the chance to express that. Or, be the guy who changed the world with her. I was not gonna disappoint her. I vowed to make a difference and be the guy who does something to make the world just a little bit better. I had to solve this case and bring to justice all those guys involved in Lolo's murder.

The bus finally pulled up to my stop. I tucked the picture away and exited through the rear door. I sprinted to the back of the Mozi house and retrieved the key to the kitchen door. Everything was exactly as it was the night before.

CHAPTER 9

I was confronted by the horror of the murder scene in the daylight. All the bloodstains were now dried and became rust in color. It was nothing like the movies I'd seen. There was a thickness in the air that weighed the room down and made me sick to my stomach. I was armed with only a key and a backpack full of puzzle pieces—notebooks, pictures, and a gaudy ring. It was time for me to get to the bottom of all of this, and decided to start in the Mozi bedroom.

Inside the room was cold. I carefully examined the room,

looking for all the least obvious of the hiding places. There had to be things hidden in plain sight, things that most adults would miss. As a kid with a nosey detective for a mother, I learned how to hide my bad grades in the cassette decks of my old radio and between dusty books that no one ever read. Where would Mozi hide his biggest secrets?

Looking under the bed, I found nothing there. Next, I checked the closet. Nothing. This room was not going to lead me anywhere. I moved on to the study. It was trashed. The guys who were in here with me the night before did not clean up after themselves at all. They checked all the obvious places, like the desk, drawers, and cabinets. What could they have missed? I noticed a picture of Lolo on what appeared to be a stand.

On approaching it to examine the picture, I noticed that there was a small opening at the top of the stand, covered only by the picture frame. I suddenly discovered that the stand contained a secret compartment.

I reached into my backpack, pulling out the small pocketknife my father had given me for protection. Then with the knife, I managed to pry open the compartment, and there it was hidden in plain sight. My eyes widened at the sight of stacks of crisp, green hundred-dollar bills. I had never seen this much money all in one place. This must be what a million dollars looks like I thought, blinking rapidly.

The guys who were here last night passed over this completely. How was I going to get al this money out of here? I decided to leave it exactly were it was and neatly put everything back as it was. Finding the money was good but it would not help me find out who killed Lolo.

I retraced my steps. Lolo did not know what her father was into, so why the key? I took the key from around my neck and held it in my hand. Why was it only her who wore this key during business meetings? Is it possible that somehow Mozi used her to keep something hidden?

Darting into Lolo's room, I began thinking about all the things she kept hidden. Her room was perfect and could probably be the best hiding place. The fact that it was so meticulously kept meant that it would not raise any suspicions.

Then I saw a trunk. It was white and covered with hearts. I opened it to find dolls and old toys. Digging through the pile, I saw a locked box. The key in my hand was the perfect fit. There it was a tiny silver digital recorder. She told me that her father would often record himself and his business partners at their secret meetings to ensure that there would always be proof of what was said. I put the recorder on my keychain along with the key to the kitchen door were it would blend in with the rest of my trinkets.

Some time in the night, I thought, I will return for the stash of money. I had to make it home before my dad started to search for me.

Exiting through the rear door, I carefully locked it behind me. Then I saw the unmarked squad car. It was a standard-issue black impala. The detectives approached me. Saying nothing they grabbed me and started dragging me to the car. They threw me up against the car and started.

"What are you doing at a closed crime scene?"

"I was just checking things out. I just wanted to see what a real crime scene looked like is all," I lied, hoping that these would be last words we shared.

"See son, we have a problem. Not only are you trespassing in an investigation but also you are breaking and entering. Anyone of these charges means jail time."

"I'm sorry, officers. I wasn't thinking. If you just let me off with a warning and let me go home, I will never do it again."

I looked directly into their eyes, pleading that I not be brought to the precinct and charged. My mom would kill me.

My heart started to palpitate and my palms were sweaty. If I were ever to be arrested, this would get me killed by both my mother and father.

"Hey Smith, should we let the kid go?" the officer asked, smiling and winking at his partner. They gazed up at the noon sun.

"I don't think so, Gatlin. It is still daytime. Shouldn't this kid be in school?"

"Well kid, guess you are taking a trip downtown," he said.

"Please don't. My mother is a detective. She would kill me if she knew I was arrested," I said in my final plea to escape.

My mom once told me that police officers looked out for their own, and using her name may come in handy if ever stopped by the police.

"Okay kid. What's your mother's name?"

"Rita Sanchez of the 402."

"You mean the one married to Stanley... Our person of interest...?"

"Yes," I said, wondering what he had to do with anything. How did they know him? He was just a teacher at some public school.

The officer's shot a glance at each other and said, "Well kid, it looks like your lucky day. We will bring you in for questioning, but we won't formally charge you. We just need some information. After you answer our questions, you will be free to go and no one has to know about our little talk."

I nodded in agreement. They opened the door and placed me in the backseat of the unmarked vehicle. As I sat in the back seat, I could feel the sunshine gleaming from the squad car. I closed my eyes and realized the amount of trouble I was in. I was in over my head, and something about these detectives did not sit right with me. Could I really trust them not to arrest me or tell my mother? Nothing made sense anymore. Why were these officers there anyway? How did they know Stanley? Come to think of it, they never even asked me my name. They did not read me my rights or search me like they do on TV. What was going on? I was at their mercy and they knew it.

The car finally pulled up to central booking on what seemed the longest ride. I felt dizzy and anxious. Deep down, I was praying hard to make it out of this situation. The detectives found an empty interrogation room. They instructed me to have a seat at the table. The chair was uncomfortable and the room felt cold. I noticed that they switched off the recording device.

Anything they were going to ask me would be off the record, not for my protection, but for theirs.

Detective Gatlin said, "Son, you have no reason to be afraid."

The door slammed shut and I could hear my heart beating loudly. I was gasping for air. It felt as if I'd been running. Why would these detectives want to speak with me? I wondered nervously taking a seat on the edge of the hard chair.

"Shareef, I want to talk to you right now about a matter that's very important. How did you come to know Mozi family?"

How did he know my name? Why did this stranger seem to know so much about us? I thought about the question, and didn't want to say anything that would get me in trouble. I decided to keep all of my answers brief. My mother always told me minors were to never be interviewed without a parent present.

Their wrinkled brows registered a high level of frustration. There was silence until one of the detectives coughed. The other cleared his throat.

"I met Lolo at school," I said before the silence returned.

"Did you say at school?" the detective asked while still coughing.

"I think that's what I heard. You knew her well?"

"Yeah," I answered.

"How well did you know her?"

"She was my best friend."

"Best friends. So I am guessing you know a lot about her and her family?"

"Not really."

"You met her family, her father and his friends, maybe?"

"No, I only hung with Lolo."

"What about Stanley and your mom? We know they 'hung out' too, right?"

"Only Stanley. My mom had nothing to do with anything," I said, trying to make sure that Mom was not implicated in whatever Stanley had going on.

"Your family would visit with Lolo's family. Both families—were they friends?"

"Stanley was friends with Mozi…" I said, letting my voice trailed. "I think I've told you all I know. May I please have some water? I'm really feeling thirsty."

"Now son, you're gonna get all the water you want, but I want my partner to hear exactly what you told me about your dad and Mr. Mozi getting along and being buddies and all."

"He's not my dad. He's my stepfather. And I told you Mr. ah…"

"Mozi, keep going…"

"They became friends and that's it," I said, throwing my hands up. "That's all I know."

"Yeah, but did you ever hear about them? Your stepfather and Mr. Mozi going on any kind of trips together?"

The detective moved a little closer as he questioned me. It made me think back to last night when my mother and stepdad were arguing. She had challenged him about the trips, and now here I was, being interrogated by the police about him.

"No, I never heard about anything like that."

My mother had told me not to lie to the police. But technically, this was not a lie. I mean, what my parents argued about last night was not really meant for my ears.

"You know son, you can go to jail for telling lies. It's called perjury. You know how long you could spend behind bars for lying to the police?"

The detective's tone changed. He was a little bit annoyed and his voice boomed loud echoing in my ear. The other detective, the one who coughed a lot, sat down and lit a cigarette. He inhaled and that made him coughed some more. The thick smoke that came out of his mouth made me want to cough. He stared at me as he smoked. The other detective ran his hand over his dome, scratched his head and shouted.

"I could tell you're lying. You do you know the police can tell when you're lying, right? I know you know that, son. So do not lie to me. Just tell me the truth and you can go home," he shouted.

"Hey partner, take it easy on the kid. Maybe he doesn't know anything else. Let up, man. Remember your heart problem. You continue like you're doing and you'll give yourself a damn heart attack. Maybe, just maybe the kid does not know anything else. He's told us all he knows. Right, kid?" he coughed as he spoke.

I glared at his frustrated partner.

"When am I gonna get out of here?" I asked.

The detective ignored me. Taking a deep, long drag of his cigarette, he inhaled deep. Then he blew smoke rings at me through a cloud of smoke.

"Ever tried one of these?" he asked, holding up a cigarette.

Lolo and I had tried to light up before. We used to imitate the posture of her father's friends talking with the cigarette dangling from their lips. Lolo would hold her glass with her pinky sticking out the way the adults did theirs.

"No," I answered nervously lying.

"Really…?" He fired back. "You wouldn't think of lying to the police, would you now?"

"No, I wouldn't lie to the police," I answered.

He stared at me expecting me to crack. I didn't know anything, I kept saying to myself.

"I know a friend of your mother's," the detective said. He inhaled then crushed the cigarette with his shoes before he continued. "This friend told me about how you tried to smoke before. It was about two months ago. Your mother caught you. This friend came to me, and told me your mother was really hot under the collar when she caught you smoking with a neighbor's kid. Now who could that have been?" the detective asked.

I closed my eyes. He knew he had caught me in a lie. My mouth felt dry as a desert and I was sick to my stomach. Looking around the room, I saw the other detective moving in closer. I sudeenly felt the urge to tell the truth. There was a long pause as I squirmed uneasily in my seat. My head was down and I stared at wood of the desk, not daring to look up at either of them. I could tell that they were both staring at me like I was the lowest form of criminal.

"Well, well. What do we have here? Are you insinuating that this kid is a liar, and has just perjured himself, detective? Let's lock him up. Are you gonna play ball or not?"

I ignored the question. I refused to cooperate.

"Shareef, you can come clean and avoid going to jail by simply telling us truthfully all you know about Mr. Mozi and your stepdad's relationship. And remember do not lie to us. Okay son?"

Finally, I raised my gaze from the desk and slowly looked at them both. I didn't know where to begin. I felt like I had committed a crime. But I didn't know what it was. Was telling lies a crime? These detectives thought it was, and at this moment, it was their game. I looked around at the room, then back to their faces.

"Come on, boy, let us know what you know. My partner already proved you're a liar. I'll have no problem locking you and your whole family up."

The mean detective was shouting. I wished I wasn't born. I refused to cry. My real father had told me never to cry no matter how loud anyone shouted at me.

"He wants to know what jail is like. Let him be."

I heard the detective's voice seeping through my thoughts.

"Now you can help her by telling us all you know."

"I'm thirsty. May I have something to drink, please?" I asked, trying to stall for an answer. These detectives were never going to let up on the questions. The detectives glance at each other. "It is not a trick question. I'm really thirsty now," I said.

The good detective nodded and the bad detective left the room. The door slammed before either of us spoke.

"You're a smart kid, Shareef. And we're not going to harm you, my partner has a hot temper. Don't you worry. I'll make sure he doesn't hurt you. But you're going to have to share everything you know with us."

The door opened and the officer walked back in. He handed me a can of Coke, and pulled the detective who was talking to me away and whispered to him. I sipped the soda, and watched nervously as they huddled in a corner away from me. I could overhear them speaking in hushed tones, and assumed they were discussing what I had told them.

Whatever the discussion was about, I really didn't know, all I know was they kept glancing over at me, scrutinizing me. Then the good detective walked back to me with a worried expression on his face. He shook his head and immediately lit a cigarette. Then pointed at me.

"You're telling me the truth, aren't you, Shareef?"

The detective appeared angry. I was confused and scared. I nodded and felt my stomach churning.

"I am telling the truth. It was just my stepfather. He was the only one going on trips with Mr. Mozi. My mother never went on any of those trips. She didn't know anything about it. She only visited them at home sometimes. We'd go visit the Mozis sometimes."

"Shareef, you can come clean and avoid going to jail by simply telling us truthfully all you know about Mr. Mozi and your stepdad's relationship. And remember do not lie to us, okay?"

"Now Shareef, you're gonna tell us the truth before my partner bursts a vein or wind up dying of a heart attack. He doesn't believe anything about patience."

My eyes wandered from the top of the desk to the expectant faces of the two detectives impatiently waiting for my answer. Even though I had eavesdropped on my parents' conversation last night and knew what they had been arguing about, I didn't say anything to the detectives. My unwillingness to part with information made them both agitated.

"Christ, maybe he doesn't understand what this means," the mean detective said. The other looked at him as if he wanted him not to.

"C'mon give him a break. Can't you see he's trying to remember all the right things? He does not want to lie to the police."

Walking over to me, the detective and asked, "Do you want a drink, kid?

I slowly shook my head then I said, "I want to go home."

Both detectives stared at me as if I had just cursed at their mothers.

"We're getting nowhere with this kid. He obviously doesn't want to talk to us. I don't care. Throw his ass in jail," the mean cop ordered.

Then he strode toward the desk, and banged his fist on its top, leaving me shaking.

"No, you're wrong. I think he wants to help us solve this thing by telling us all he knows. He doesn't want to see his mother in handcuffs and going to jail. Do you, Shareef?" the good detective asked.

"All you gotta do is cooperate with us. We're the good guys. Remember? Those friends of your mother and father, I mean stepfather are the bad guys. And they're the ones who caused your friend to be killed. Are you listening to me?" the detective asked.

I nodded and felt an uneasy feeling creeping up from the pit of my stomach. It remained stuck in my throat, and made speaking impossible. I was feeling faint until I heard the detective's voice.

"She should not have died," he continued.

It was uncomfortable thinking of Lolo dying. We were good friends, and if I could do something to help the situation I would. I heard the detective's voice seeping through my thoughts.

"Now you can help her by simply telling us all you know."

His voice was reassuring, but it was what the detective *wasn't* saying that caused me to break down and cry. I started thinking about my mother in handcuffs and all because of something that my stepfather did.

My teeth chattered and my body shook nervously. I couldn't continue.

"Don't be scared," the detective said, handing me a cigarette. I declined. "Ha, ha," he laughed. "You don't have to be shy around us, Shareef. Shareef, we'll let you go, but you've got to cooperate with us." The detective stared menacingly at me and his faced reddened as he hurled threats. "There are all kinds of mean guys in the joint who can't wait to tear you a new—"

"All right. Let's take it easy on the kid,"

We were in the office. As I sat at the desk, I nervously glanced over the photos while the two detectives waited for an answer.

Suddenly the door was flung opened, and things got crazy up in there. My dad stood at the entrance with his fists clenched. I read *LOVE* and *HATE* tattooed on his fists.

"What the hell is going on here?" he shouted. "I know my rights, and my son ain't supposed to be here. He's only eleven and questioning him without his parents being here is illegal. I'm gonna call the DA, the mayor, the newspapers. Everybody is gonna hear about this. Heads gonna roll. Let me see some badges. Because when I'm through suing—"

"Who are you supposed to be, mister? Who gave you permission to interfere in official police business?"

"What? What? How dare you arrest my son, treating him like he's some sort of common criminal? Y'all in here illegally questioning him and all. No way, that's right. He's a minor! And y'all know that ain't right."

"You got some ID on you?" one of the detectives calmly asked.

He moved menacingly closer to my father. There was a lot of tension in the air. My dad wasn't giving an inch. Something had to give. I could sense that it was going to happen way before it did, but I felt paralyzed. I couldn't do anything except closed my eyes. My father attempted to look at the detective's badge, and as soon as he did, the detective signaled to the officers, who were already in position behind my dad, to take him down.

He had been standing with his back to the entrance and did not see the sea of blue uniforms behind him. In no time, they had him in cuffs and led him away with his wrists bleeding. The detective slammed the door.

"How the hell—how did he get in here? I thought there was a lieutenant at the desk?"

"There was an officer at the desk. I'll go check out what caused the breakdown."

Detective Smith walked out, leaving me with the mean Detective Brown. My blood chilled when he looked at me. He seemed to want to end my life right then and there. Fear ran through me and I looked away, not wanting to hold eye contact with the scary detective.

"Now your father's temper has put you in a bind. You saw him attack me. Now he's going to be charged with resisting arrest, obstruction of justice, as well as assaulting a police officer. But you can start helping not only yourself but also that stupid father of yours."

The detective stared at me. I sat more nervous than before and all that kept flashing through my mind was how quickly my father was taken out and how bloody he was. They had beaten him down. The detective must have read my mind because he immediately shouted at me.

"Hey kid, don't ignore me! Now your father is an adult. He knows he cannot bloody well behave in that manner at a police precinct. He will go to jail. The question is, do you want to save him?"

"I do. I don't want him to go to jail," I said, shuddering and pleading for my father's freedom. "He was just angry, that's all."

He whispered something to the other detective, and they walked out together. I was too tired to care and closed my eyes. It was about an hour before they returned. Smith walked over and shook my shoulder. I was startled and jumped. He was fingering a folder filled with photos.

The thought of what happened to my dad made my weary bones rattle so loud I couldn't hear either detective as they huddled. Where did they put dad? I wondered. Did they arrest him? I kept thinking of how long would the torture last, I felt trapped and had to do something that would get my father and me out of this place.

"You can help us find her killer or killers by looking at this folder."

I glanced at the folder without opening it, thinking this was all about obtaining information on the Mozi family. I had lost my best friend to some of the men who were at her father's party. I turned to the first page of the folder, and saw that some of the faces looked familiar, but I wasn't sure anymore.

The detectives checked their watches and carefully observed my reaction. I purposely pointed to each face I remembered seeing at parties thrown at the Mozis'. After I fingered about eight faces, the detectives nodded and smiled.

"Now that's much better. All you gotta do now is tell us about your mother's and—uh—your stepdad's involvement, and I'd say we're making unbelievable progress. Wouldn't you agree with that, Detective Smith?"

"I'd say you're right. But…"

"Why is there a 'but' detective?"

"How can we trust what he's saying? The boy might just be lying to get his daddy off the hook."

"How can we trust you?" Detective Brown asked.

"I'm telling the truth. I swear. I'm not lying."

The folder was snatched and I watched the detectives racing from the office. The door slammed shut and I laid my head on the desk. My tears formed a puddle in my lap. I didn't care.

I closed my eyes wishing my nightmare would end. In the quiet office, loneliness and fear were my only companions, and they offered no comfort. Every footstep I heard made me cringe. There was no relief when my thoughts shifted to the beat-down dad had suffered at the hands of too many cops to count.

It happened so quickly he never even knew what hit him. In a flash he was arrested. Were they coming back to give me a similar beat-down? My mind was exhausted from trying to block the thought.

Anxiety crept back and grew stronger with each silhouette outside the opaque glass door. I worried they were going to do the same thing to me once they found out I was lying.

"Good. Now that you are telling the truth, we can finally start getting some real answers." The detective said, seating himself across from me. His shoulders lowered and his eyes pierced mine. It was as if we were the only ones in the room. He became almost romantic in his tone. "Tell me something, Shareef, has your stepfather planned on going to the police?"

"Yes," I answered. I thought to myself that these cops should know that since my mother was taking him in for questioning today. Did Stanley mention what he might be saying to the police? What kind of information would he be sharing?

"I'm not sure what you are asking me."

The detective seemed to become agitated all over again and asked, "Is he cooperating with the investigation?"

"No he did not want anything to do with the police."

Why would cops be asking me this? I broke the eye contact between the detective and myself and looked down at the table. In the reflection of the mirrored effect caused by the shiny metal surface, I saw the ring. The same ring Stanley and Mr. Mozi had. This was not an investigation, but rather an effort to find out what's going to happen to them. This ring must mean something. These guys must be involved.

"Are you sure, kid? Are you telling the truth?"

"Yes, I am telling the truth."

"Alright kid, I'm going to let you out of here. We can keep this little talk between us private. Remember we could have arrested you for breaking and entering, along with trespassing.

"Understood," I said.

I just wanted to get out before any other surprise found me, but it was just not supposed to be that way.

CHAPTER 10

"Is my mother here?" I asked.

There were no immediate answers, but I was sure that it was the voice of my mother coming to my rescue. Or perhaps I was just imagining things? I could feel a headache growing when the idea that I could have imagined hearing my mother's voice hit me. I sat back in the chair. Then I heard the voice again.

"Shareef, Shareef, Shareef..."

I felt warmth oozing through my body. I was alive again.

I could finally hear my mother's comforting voice.

"Where is my son?" she asked.

"Mom, I'm in here," I immediately answered.

Hope had returned and I waited, but the door didn't pop wide open. Disappointment carved me like I was a well-done turkey ready for Thanksgiving meal. I held my breath, scared to even think of going out there. They could say I was trying to escape and could easily shoot me. The voices grew louder and I had to be sure one of them was my mother's. I carefully wrapped my hands around the knob so it wouldn't squeak and slowly pulled the door opened. Forcing one eye shut, I spied down the hallway. I couldn't see much, but I could hear the voices clearer.

"Where's my son? His father left me a message that he was not at school. I shouldn't expect any better from him—he never lives up to his responsibilities. Just wait until I see him." I could hear my mother's voice coming through loud and clear.

Elated, I jumped into the hallway and shouted, "Mom I'm right here!"

There was no answer. I did not see anyone. Was I going crazy? I felt sick, my heart dropped. Desperately I took off and started searching the hallways.

"What're you doing here?"

I heard the voice and whirled to see a police officer staring me down. I quickly glanced around to see where the others were. There were none. It was just I, and the officer standing before me. I quickly thought of an answer.

"I, uh… wanted to use the bathroom," I lied.

He looked me up and down before he said, "There is one at that end of the hall." He pointed in the other direction.

"Thank you, sir," I said then turned to go.

"Hey kid, I'll go with you. You're gonna need the code for the door."

My heart froze for a second. I was trying to get away from these police and now this man in uniform wanted to walk me to the bathroom.

"Oh, I don't need to use the bathroom anymore…"

"It's not a problem, kid. I'm not in a hurry, and besides police officers aren't mean people. What—are you in school?"

"Uh-huh…"

"What're you—like ten years old or something like that?"

"Uh-huh…"

"The guns aren't scaring you, right? You've seen a real gun before, haven't you?"

"Uh-huh…"

"Where did you see real guns? Your friends have real guns?"

"No, his mother has real guns. Can you please tell me what's going on?"

The question hung in the air. The officer fumbled for an answer as I ran in the arms of my mother. I was going to be all right.

"I found him wandering the hallway. He told me he was looking for the bathroom, lieutenant. I was just escorting him there so I could open the door for him. I mean I could have brought him…"

"Everything is under control at this point, officer. Thank you," the lieutenant said.

"You take care, kid," the officer said as he walked away.

I was holding my mother's hand real tight. I glanced up at her face and I could tell from the look in her eyes she was really getting angry.

"Lieutenant Mullins, you're the desk officer can you tell me what has been happening to my son?" My mother asked. She was wearing a badge around her neck and held onto it as she spoke. "I mean if my son was arrested, why wasn't I informed?

And if so, just what was he arrested for? I don't understand. Can I see the pedigree sheet please…? You know what—forget about it. Just give me a minute and let me talk to my son."

"You can use the office on the other end of the hallway," the lieutenant said.

"Okay, thank you," my mother said. She turned to me. "Let's go in the office so I can find out what's going on, Shareef."

The suggestion seemed harmless enough but it suddenly stirred up a feeling of dread for me. My feet were reluctant to move forward.

"Shareef, what's the matter with you? Both you and that man I call my husband have already caused enough problems for one day. Now you're going inside this office and we're going to talk about your little problem and being arrested."

It was plain to me that my mother was getting angrier with me by the second. Still clutching her hand, I apprehensively walked down the hallway. I knew I was in a lot of trouble, but at least my mother was here next to me.

I was now being forced to remember what had happened all over again. As my mind spiraled through the day thinking about the fight in the lunchroom, my subsequent arrest and my father getting beaten up and being arrested, all my hopes plummeted.

Standing outside the door, I braced myself for the worst. My mother opened the door and it dawned on me that getting out of this mess was not going to be a cakewalk.

"Sit over there, Mister man," she ordered.

I glanced at the desk in the corner with the chair of torture waiting for me. I didn't want to go back through the grueling ritual even though my mother was now in charge.

"Mom, do I have to sit over there? I could stand right here, can't I?" I asked nervously.

"Yes, sit right over there, and do not start with your questions. I'm doing all the questioning around here, okay. You got that, Shareef?"

With her finger pointing punitively at me, I knew that my mother was not about to take any slack from me. I had waited anxiously to leave this place, now my mother forcefully brought me back. Nothing was going right up to this point. I had miscalculated what my mother's reaction would be.

Unwillingly, I walked to the desk under the scrutiny of my mother's glare searing through my back. It was pressure time and I began to think of how it all started. My thoughts were blocked by a stubborn mind that would not let me think of anything but the present situation. I sat down and awaited my mother's questions.

"Shareef, I read the police arrest report. You cut school? Trespassed at a crime scene? What is going on with you?"

"Mom, it wasn't…"

"Don't you appreciate what I'm doing for you? I have a job. First your stepdad is arrested for smuggling drugs and now you're arrested at the same time. What am I supposed to do? Your father doesn't support us, and I have got to do this alone it is getting too stressful for me—"

I looked at my mother and saw the tears streaming down her face. I wanted to hug her but she turned her back and walked away. I waited listening to her heavy breathing. She unfolded a sheet of paper and read it for a few seconds then she gazed at me.

"I'm sorry, mommy. I never meant to cause any trouble."

"Then what is it then, Shareef?" she asked, sounding annoyed.

"I don't know, mom."

"You don't know? Now that's a great answer, mister man. As a matter of fact that's a fantastic answer. You know you're never ever going to play a second of video game until you're eighteen? You know that don't you?"

It seemed like my whole world had fell apart. "You know, Shareef, you're always blaming someone else."

That was it. My life was over. Eighteen, I thought. That was too long. She had to be kidding. Yes, she was only doing what the detectives were trying to do. My mother was trying to scare me. I guess that was better than going to jail.

"Mom, I'm not going to lie to you."

"Why didn't your father come for you?" she asked.

"He did, mom. He came here when those detectives were questioning me. We were right here in this office."

"Shareef, are you for real? When was your father here?"

"Hours ago and they had him arrested."

"Are you making this up? I mean you're in enough trouble already. Don't push your luck," she said, wagging her finger at me.

"I swear, mom, I am telling the truth. Dad came and he was mad the two detectives had me here alone. He got real mad and started yelling then..."

"Wait a minute, Shareef. Your father was here?"

"I swear..."

"And he was arrested by two detectives who were questioning you?"

"Yeah, that's what happened."

"I don't get this. Why would detectives question you, and about what?"

"They came and got me from the other place."

"What other place are you talking about, Shareef?"

"Mom when they brought me here, they took off the handcuffs and made me fill out a questionnaire about what happened, then they made me sign the form."

"You did what?" My mother's face reddened with anger. She glared at me. "What were those detectives questioning you about, Shareef? I want the truth, Shareef."

"Mommy, listen I didn't tell them anything. They wanted to know about the parties that I uh… attended at uh, you know…"

"No, I don't know, Shareef."

"They wanted me to tell them who I had seen at the parties and asked me if you and uh…"

"Those bastards!"

My mother's scream scared me. For a minute, I thought I was in a heap of trouble again. I felt like urinating. I wanted to ask her to leave the room and use the bathroom, but couldn't bring myself to ask. She was obviously very angry and I did not want her anger coming back at me.

"The detectives kept asking and asking, but I said nothing. They showed me pictures of all these men and I just kept my mouth shut."

"Those rotten bastards will not get away with this! Shareef, stay here and I'll be right back. I need to go have a chat with the lieutenant at the desk."

Mother slammed the door and walked out, leaving me sitting at the dreaded desk to wonder what she was about to do.

CHAPTER 11

I was feeling relieved that my mother's anger was now directed toward someone other than myself. She had a rough day. I had been arrested my father and stepfather were also arrested. Everything seemed to have gone wrong for her. I jumped when I heard her voice sounding angry and loud. I got up and walked to the door. Carefully, I tried strained to peek at what was going on.

"I don't give a damn. You're a lieutenant at the desk and you know that if a minor is arrested you have to make every effort to contact the parents or guardian of the child. You don't give permission to anyone to question the child. You're a female lieutenant, for heaven's sake! Do you have a child?"

"Look, you've got to understand—I had no control. I came to the desk and saw the pedigree sheet filled out. I thought the arresting officers had your son in their custody. I didn't know he was being questioned. I don't have that on any official records. I don't know—maybe your son is making up a story. You know, kids do embellish. They're just like adults. They'll do or say anything to get out of trouble."

That was not the truth and I had to do something to let my mother know. I ran out the door to where both my mother and the officer stood. They turned and stared wide-eyed at me.

"I didn't make it up, mommy! Two detectives they had me in that office right there," I said and pointed at the dreaded office door.

"Young man…" the police officer started, but I quickly interrupted.

"Yes, two detectives came and took me in there and showed me pictures and asked me to identify these men. They asked me about my mother and one of them said that he was your good friend, mommy. I trusted them. Then they kept me in there and my father came in and they beat him up and…

and locked him up. One detective said he was interfering with official business. And they charged him with resisting arrest."

"How long were you inside the office with the detectives, Shareef?"

"It was like two or three hours."

I was not sure anymore. The more I thought about it, the more things melded all together like one big nightmare. The day had left an unforgettable imprint on my mind. Events wound into a tighter knot in my brain.

The look of anguish on my mother's face put a question in my conscience. Did she believe or not? She seemed tormented by doubts. Law enforcement was her career. I know my mother wanted to believe the lieutenant but then I heard her asked the question that removed all doubts.

"You had my son here and knew that these detectives were illegally questioning and you did nothing to stop it?" mother asked.

The officer standing next to her gazed at me then things started getting better for me as I heard my mother started barking orders.

"I'm going to file some complaints. I want to know the names of the detectives involved. I want to speak to the arresting officers and I want a copy of the pedigree sheet they filed after they arrested my son. I also want to see the complaint against my son that warranted his arrest and I want all this right now, lieutenant!"

"Calm down…"

"What do you mean, 'calm down'?"

"Look officer, hear me out. Moments ago you asked me if I've got children. I raised three boys and a girl right here in this city. One night I got a telephone call saying that my youngest boy had been arrested for possession of controlled substance. I had to get out of bed and go get my son out of lockup. The arresting officer found him hanging with a group of teens that had been loud and drinking. The officers searched everyone and found a bag of weed on my son. The next day I had to go back to work and show my face to all my colleagues."

"What's your point?" mother asked.

"I empathize with what you're going through and I know about embarrassment on the job. The career you've chosen is one that calls for your objectivity in all circumstances. Detectives may have been out of line. But take it on the chin and tomorrow will be a better day for you. Fussing with them over that situation may be a big mistake."

"How could you say that would be a big mistake? They had my child secluded, and interrogated on things they had no right talking to him about, even if I was standing right next to him. And now you're telling me to calm down. You should be ashamed to call yourself a mother."

"I'm only doing my job."

"Lieutenant, do your job by getting me all the information that I requested, alright? That is your job right now."

"Look, you don't have to make this into something it isn't. The police department is made up of people, and people do make mistakes sometimes. You should understand."

"Look lieutenant, if you don't get me everything that I have requested pronto, I'm going above your head to get it. So you best get to stepping, lieutenant."

"Please listen to me and do not make this mistake," the lieutenant said, pleading with my mother, and for an eternity she considered it. I could see her mind going over her choices.

"Lieutenant, please do as I asked," my mother quietly said.

She looked completely composed and the quiet assertive energy she exuded made me strong. I felt happy that she was my mother and I knew that she had to make a difficult decision. She had chosen family over career.

I recognized it but could not fully comprehend what it took to make such a decision. One way or another, my mother was set to take a loss.

I stood watching as she carefully checked the logbooks on the desk. Once she slipped her badge around her neck, not only her posture but also her entire appearance changed, she became determined.

Wrong or right, she had to prove something had gone awry. I watched as she read each and every syllable, examining sheet after sheet of paper. Then she walked over to where I stood with my breath coming in gasps.

"Did you sign any papers when you were arrested?" she asked.

I nodded.

"Is this one of them?" I nodded again.

"Did you write everything on this paper?" she asked, shoving the paper in my face. "Please read it carefully, Shareef."

She walked away to a copy machine and ran copies of the other paper she was carrying. I slowly and methodically read the one she had left in my hand. It contained some of the things that I had said and some that I had not. I would warn mother about this discrepancy.

The stench of this place was getting to me, but when mother walked back to me I felt safer. She took the sheet and came closer so she could stare into my eyes. She must have seen something.

"We'll talk when we get out of here, son," she said.

I felt like I was a part of something that was known exclusively to my mother and me. She finished copying all the papers and then we walked out hand in hand. It gave me a thrill when my mother and I silently left sharing a secret.

When we hit the streets I felt a breath of fresh air whipping around me. My mother opened the car door and I got in next to her. She put the key in the ignition and I began to think of finally going home.

"I know you're hungry, Shareef. How about we stop at Friendly's restaurant, huh?" she suggested.

"Sounds really good, mom," I said with a smile that stretched from ear to ear.

As mother drove along I began to feel better about my chances at proving that I was an innocent victim in all that had happened today. Mom wore a tight look of concern on her face. Maybe she was trying to sort out all the details in her mind. I was finally able to smile when she searched for parking.

"Okay, are you ready to eat, Shareef?" she asked.

"You bet, mom," I answered.

We exited the car and walked inside. The place was not crowded. Mom and I ordered burgers. Her cell phone rang.

"Oh hi, mother," I heard her say and knew it was my father's mother. She always called her "Mother."

"Excuse me a second, Shareef," she said, looking at me, then went back to listening to my grandmother. "He's going to be fine. He'll be all right. Well, what do you expect when a person acts up? You know your son. He doesn't listen to anyone."

Our sodas arrived. Mother stirred and I sipped while she listened to my grandmother. The food came next. I overheard mother trying graciously to get grandmother off the phone.

"I'm about to have something to eat with Shareef. I'll call you back. And stop worrying, your son will be all right. They're going to release him on a ROR. He'll probably have to see the judge, but it shouldn't be too bad. He has a right to sue. I'll call you later. Shareef is fine he's chomping down on a burger. Your grandmother says she loves you and will see you soon, Shareef. Bye, mother. Love you too."

My mother hung up and just as soon as she touched her

burger, her phone rang again.

"Ignore it, mom." She looked at me, glared and picked up the phone.

"Hello, Brenda..."

That would be my stepfather's ex-wife. She was the young-at-heart type and liked to be called by her first name, even by me.

"I'm having dinner with Shareef and I really can't speak right now but I'll call you later and we'll talk. I promise. Shareef, Brenda sends you hugs and kisses."

"Same to her," I managed between bites.

"Shareef sends lots of hugs and kisses to you. I'll talk to you later Brenda, bye-bye."

Mother ended the call and returned to her burger. She took a bite and again her phone rang. She looked at it and immediately identified the number. "It's your grandma." She announced before answering. "Yes, huh-uh, I know but I can't talk right now. Why? Because I'm having dinner with your grandson, that's why." I heard mother speaking emotionally and knew it was her mother. "Not now, Mommy, I'll call you when I get home, okay. I promise."

I was busy eating fries when she put the phone down and

took a bite of her burger. She shook her head and I knew it had not been an enjoyable day for neither of us.

"How's the burger, mom?"

"If I am allowed to eat it, I could tell you," she smiled and I knew she was making light of a bad thing.

Mother had the ability to do so. When she and dad had argued, she had still been able to smile. Today she seemed even stronger and younger. She was like a friend sharing a private joke with me. Maybe this was a chance for us to get closer.

"Enjoy your burger, mommy."

"Thank you, son," she said.

The look she gave me told another story. I didn't want to ask because eventually she would share it. She looked weary now, slowly chewing the burger while quickly sinking deep into her thoughts. Mother sipped and burped. It seemed that my father's arrest made some sense of the whole incident. My mother finished eating without saying a word. There was more to her silence than the air it gave. I breathed hard hoping to draw attention to myself. Mother threw a glance my way but seemed miles away in thought. Clearly there had been more to her day than just me getting arrested. I decided the only way to find out what else happened was to bother her and ask.

"I know it wasn't a good day for you and I am partly to blame for that. I am sorry, mommy."

She looked at me with sad eyes.

"I'm sorry, mommy," I repeated in my most earnest voice.

My mother finally gazed at me instead of through me.

"Your apology is accepted, Shareef. Please just don't let it happen again."

"I swear…I mean, I promise never ever to let it happen again."

She held my hand as she cautioned me. "You're a chip off the old block and sometimes you have a tendency to act out. Let today be a lesson and warning to you, Shareef. The next time it may not go down this way."

I nodded and walked around the table to hug my mother.

"Is there something else bothering you, mommy?" I asked as I clutched my mother's shoulders. She knelt down and looked me in the eyes.

"It's grown-up business and much too complicated for you, Shareef. But thanks for asking. It's something that only I can work out right now. You're too cute when you want to be, Shareef. Let's pay and go home."

Minutes later we were walking hand in hand to the parking lot when I spotted a van of officers. Some wore uniforms and others didn't. They waved at us and I felt anxiety crawling beneath my skin as they approached.

"Hi Rita, how're you doing?"

"Hey guys, who's in charge of this task force?"

"Why?" one of the men asked.

"I just wanna know if this break is an emergency?"

They laughed and hugged and shook hands with mother.

"Shareef, meet the only unit I was not qualified to be part of," she laughed. "But my partner went instead."

One of the team members stepped forward. He kissed mother and reached out his hand to me.

"Hi son, my name is Carlos Ramirez. You could call me Charlie. I'm guilty as charged," he smiled.

I glanced up at him, and realized that he too was sporting the same ring that the detectives, Stanley and Mr. Mozi had. He was not to be trusted. I don't know what came over me then. I started to sweat, my head felt heavier and my feet seemed not want to go any further. I wanted to say something to my mother but the words stayed stuck in my throat.

"What's wrong, Shareef?" my mother asked.

"Are you alright, boy?"

The officers got closer and I grabbed my stomach like a lion was trapped inside. Instinctively I gripped my mother's hand tightly. She seemed confused and shot me a look of bewilderment.

"Shareef, you don't feel well?" she asked.

"You better take care of your boy, Rita."

"Is there something wrong?" she asked.

Wincing, I shook my head. The officers looked on in concern. Then they smiled at my mother, looked down menacingly at me and walked away.

"Shareef, are you okay?"

I wanted to tell her everything I discovered in the last twenty-four hours, but my voice failed me. Not able to take my eyes off the officers, I pointed in fear as they got near. This weird feeling hit me and I couldn't bring myself to formulate words. I felt nauseated and shivered like I was in a freezer.

"Shareef, Shareef, are you all right? Is everything okay?" she asked. The inquiry lingered embarrassingly in the air.

"C'mon Shareef, let's get home," my mother said.

She grabbed my hand and started pulling me. Tentatively, I tried to move while keeping my butt cheeks close together to prevent further leakage. I was petrified and moved forward unwillingly alongside my startled mother.

CHAPTER 12

During the ride home I was quiet. Mother's face was all concern as she rushed me home, all the time asking questions. Her mind stayed in overdrive. I was still feeling embarrassed from the experience, and desperately wanted to block it out.

"Are you feeling any better, Shareef?" mother asked when she caught my stare. I shook my head. "Shareef, are you ignoring me? Shareef, answer me."

I heard my mother's request but was too mortified to come out of the cocoon I had wrapped myself into. We drove closer to home and I saw the yellow tape marking the crime scene of the killings.

The Mozis' home, once the best on the block, was now reduced to a house of haunting ghosts. I had to confess all the things I saw in that house, all the evidence stashed in my bags, the rings—everything—but would she believe me? Or maybe she would just be mad that I went poking my nose in what she called 'grown folks' business? My throat tightened and my breathing increased. I sank into the seat and my fist clung to the door.

"Why are you acting this way, Shareef?"

"What do you mean? I don't know, mom."

"Shareef, earlier outside Friendly's you seemed, alright until…" Her voice trailed and then she shrugged. "I don't know what is wrong, Shareef."

"Mom, I've got something to tell you, but I don't know if you are going to believe me."

"Shareef, I'm your mother. You know you can talk to me."

"Last night after the funeral, I went to the Mozi house."

"You did what? Shareef…!"

"Mom, please just hear me out. Before you get all upset

just listen."

"Okay, Shareef. You have my attention."

"Last night when I went to the house—at first, I just really wanted to get a picture of Lolo and say goodbye. But while I was there some men arrived. They were searching for something. So today, I cut class and went back to see what I could find." I reached for my backpack and pulled out everything I had collected from the house. I pulled out the ring.

"Mom, this ring—all the guys involved in Lolo's murder have it. Mozi, the two detectives who interrogated me, your friend Charlie, and even Stanley..."

"What? It's just a ring, Shareef. You are acting as if there is some major conspiracy. Do you hear what you are saying? Sneaking out at night, cutting school—now you want to tell these wild stories and lie about my partner and my husband!"

"Mom, please. You have got to believe me. Something is not right and it is pointing to Stanley. The detectives who questioned me today were asking me if Stanley was 'cooperating with the police.' They picked me up only to see what we knew and if Stanley was a snitch."

"Nonsense Shareef! I don't want to hear anymore of this. You go to your room."

"But mom, please Just look at this stuff. Look at it. You are a cop. This is evidence. Just look at it, please."

"I said go to your room now, Shareef! I'm going to make an appointment with the psychiatrist for you, boy. Who do you think you are, Sherlock Holmes or something? That boy es loco," she whistled.

I wasn't going to stick around because that look in her eyes yold me all I needed to hear. She was not listening. She could not hear me over the blue uniforms, the marriage license, and the bond between her and her partner. My mom was loyal and would not be won over with evidence from the likes of me, her kid who had snuck out, and cut class.

The phone rang and she turned her back to get it. My mother began speaking and quickly I realized the coast was clear. I scuttled off to my room.

"Hello Brenda," I heard my mother saying as I jumped into my pajamas and dashed into bed. My stepfather's ex was calling again.

The place was awfully quiet without Stanley around. My breathing and the voice of my mother on the phone were the only things I could hear.

"He's being held as a potential witness. They had to

provide him with protective custody. I'll let him know you'll be going to your mother's in Charlotte. Huh-uh, its precautionary measures they're taking because Mr. Mozi was ambushed and killed after he decided to cooperate with the investigation.... Yes they're holding him in safekeeping. Brenda, I have to go. Good night."

That night, I was on my back in bed staring at the ceiling fan, and thinking about what to do next. I would have to quit the investigation before it got me into any more trouble. My mother and I may never know the truth. She could end up staying with Stanley and losing her life because of who and what he was caught up with. I decided to keep everything in my backpack and carry it with me at all times no matter where I went. Soon, it would all be revealed somehow. My thoughts would not be denied, and my eyes would not close.

CHAPTER 13

The next morning my mother took me to my grandma's place. She felt it best I stay there so someone could watch me twenty-four-seven. Stanley's legal situation really had her preoccupied. She seemed really on edge.

My cousin, Tito was there with aunt Lila. She was my mother's older sister and had been recently divorced. They were living with grandma until my aunt could find her own apartment. It worked out well even though I was suspended from school. During the day when everyone was gone, I was alone with my grandma. I would do homework until it was time for her to watch the soaps on TV and didn't want to be bothered.

"Now Shareef, you go play with your video games and after that we'll continue doing your school work," she said dismissing me.

"Okay, grandma."

I went in the room where my cousin stayed and wild out on the video games. Tito and I were a year apart. He had the same games I did, and much more. Hours later, I was so involved that I didn't even hear when grandmother called me.

"Shareef, boy, come and get something to eat. Your mom will be here soon."

The doorbell rang, and grandma went to get it. It was Tito getting home from school. That meant it was time to have fun on the video game again. Mother and Aunty Lila, I called her Tita Lila, arrived about an hour later.

"Shareef, let's go," she said, foregoing her usual greeting of a hug. Mother was rushing me out, when grandma interceded.

"Rita, why don't you let Shareef eat? That boy has not let up since I gave him breakfast. What is it about these games?"

"Okay, but Shareef should know better. And you mommy, letting him do what he wants to do, that just ain't gonna work."

"Shareef and Tito go and eat the food I made you. Lila warm up the rice and beans for Shareef and Tito," my grandma shouted.

"Come on and get it boys," Aunty Lila said.

Tito and I walked to the kitchen. I saw the frown on mother's face.

"I can't wait for him to go back to school," she said.

"That'll happen next week," grandma said, sitting down. "Tell me, what's really eating you?"

"It's really nothing, Ma. You're soo nosey," my mother laughed.

"Now, you're my daughter—you best believe I can tell when something is bothering you, girl," grandma said.

I joined my cousin and aunt in the kitchen and ate.

"C'mon Shareef, you better get some of this before Tito eats it all," my aunt said, ushering me into a chair.

"Mommy, I can't eat all this food grandma cooked. There's enough for all of us."

"Stop the chatter, bow your head, say your grace and dig in," Aunt Lila smiled.

We chow down on beans and rice with chicken. After that, Tito and I walked in on the adults. They were lost in deep discussion sitting in the living room.

"Mommy, can we play video games until I'm ready to do my homework?" Tito asked.

"No, you've got school tomorrow and…"

"Lila, don't be so hard on the boy. Let him and Shareef play their game for a few more minutes," grandma said objecting.

"All right, but you heard your grandma—just for a few minutes. Not all night,"

"Now tell me what that therapist is saying. My grandson isn't crazy. You know I saw Dr. Santiago the other day…"

"That man is handsome, mommy! You should've married that man," Aunt Lila said. My grandmother, aunt and mother all laughed.

"Speaking of handsome, Lenny called earlier today. He was released and was inquiring about Shareef. He wanted to spend time with him, he said."

"Lenny can forget about me ever leaving my son with him unsupervised again."

"Yeah mommy, he should swap some of his good looks, and become a more responsible father. Kids go in the room, please," Aunt Lila said.

Tito and I went back to his room and we started a new

round of video games.

The weekend came and my dad called twice trying to reach mother. Both times it felt good for some reason to let him know she was unavailable. I never mentioned this to Grandma or Mother. Monday approached with the quickness. It was my first day back to school and mother seemed relieved as she rushed me off.

"Shareef, let's go," she said.

I ran down the stairs, grabbed my book bag and joined her in the car.

"Buckle up," she ordered.

I did, and she took off driving past the Mozis'. There was always a police officer or two on guard. My stomach did loops, but I couldn't really tell if it was caused by seeing them, or anticipating what would happen at school.

"Please do not get into any type of trouble whatsoever, Shareef. There are times when you should know when to fight or not to. Those school people are waiting for you to mess up. Please do not give them the satisfaction, okay, Shareef?"

"Yes mom," I said, keeping my head straight.

"Look at me, Shareef. Promise Mommy you will be a good boy," she said as the car rolled to a stop outside the school.

"I promise, mommy."

"Okay, let's go."

Mother walked with me to the office and waited until I was sent off to join my class.

"Remember your promise to me, Shareef," she reminded.

I smiled and walked out the office. It was less than quiet in the class on my return. The room was abuzz. Most of my classmates greeted me as if I was some sort of a rock star. The attention didn't go over well with any of the teachers. They acted as if I was about to pull out a gun and stick them all up. This overly cautious attitude by the teachers added to my reputation. I spent the whole day trying to play it all down. Finally, when school ended I had the chance to escape.

I waited outside for my mother. She was later than her normal half hour. The time was slowly inching toward the hour when the assistant principal invited me back inside.

"Shareef," she shouted.

I heard, but pretended I didn't.

"Shareef," she said, raising her voice louder. "I have a message from your mother."

I immediately turned and looked at her. As we were walking back to the most miserable place on earth, my mind churned. Why would my mother make me stay here? Before I knew it, I was sitting in the office, watching the witches speaking on phones.

"Shareef, your mother called and said she would be late. You may sit there and do your homework. Arrangements are being made to get someone else to pick you up."

"Thank you, Miss Brown," I said.

"All right Shareef, you're welcome. Too bad your father is in jail, but then that jail thing seems to run in the family I see."

I stared at her without saying anything. Her ugly mug held my gaze for a few minutes too long and I glared.

I removed a textbook from my book bag and buried my head in it.

Sitting alone in the room felt like being in detention. Time dragged by slowly. Eventually I heard my mother's voice.

"Hey Shareef, are you ready to go?"

"More than ready," I said.

We walked quickly out of the building to the car. I watched her hoping she would speak. She didn't. We drove in silence past the Mozi home, where police officers were out. My mother turned her head to see as she drove by.

"Wow," I said letting up my window and slumping down

in the seat. "Mom, why are there so many police there?" I asked.

The uneasiness in my tone seemed to confuse her. My mother stared at me before saying.

"Shareef just cut out the drama. Those guys are investigators from the crime lab."

When we reached our driveway, I raced from the car to the bathroom. I could feel my mother's eyes following me all the way up the stairs.

"Shareef, we have to talk when you come downstairs."

I heard her but had already slammed the door to the bathroom. Later, I came down not knowing what to expect. Mother was waiting for me. She seemed pensive and nervous. Her hands patted the seat on the sofa next to her.

"Honey, things are gonna change…"

Speechless, I waited.

"Shareef, I'm talking about…" she started speaking, but her voice stalled as if she was having difficulty saying what she wanted to communicate.

"What is it, mommy?"

"We're going to take care of that," she said, gulped air, sighed and continued. "You've got to go and live with grandma for a while. The trial—at the trial, your stepfather decided to cooperate with the prosecutors. It was the right thing for him to do."

I listened intently not really comprehending the magnitude of the dilemma.

"I—your stepfather and I, we're not seeing eye to eye on this, Shareef. Needless to say, because of the situation he's currently in, he has no choice. He has to cooperate with the investigators."

"What about dad?" I asked.

"Your dad…? Now there's another crazy one. He's gonna be held for a few days to teach him a lesson and then released."

"But he was just trying to be helpful and get me out."

"Please Shareef!"

"Okay mommy, I'll cooperate with you and go to grandma's. When do I leave?"

"Tonight," she said.

We ate dinner and she helped me pack my clothes. With all my drawers were empty, it was like I wasn't ever coming back. I took all my games, too. Maybe I wouldn't need them all but I took them anyway. I helped lug the bags into the car. My room appeared empty when I returned for a final check.

"No way am I going to do that, Lenny. He's gonna stay

with Mother. You and those lawyers can do what you want. I'm not going to put Shareef's life in danger. Please do not call my mother harassing her. Good night, Lenny."

Mother hung up the phone as I made my way downstairs. There were no bags packed for mother.

"Aren't you coming with me to grandma's?" I asked as we walked out.

"No," my mother said, shaking her head slowly. "I'll be staying with your stepfather. Shareef, honey, I don't want you to be afraid, but promise me you'll be real careful when you go and stay at grandma's, okay?"

"Okay mommy, I promise."

"That's my boy," she said and gave me a kiss. "Now, Shareef, please call my cell if there are any problems," she said, handing me a cell phone. "Here take this. It's my backup line, and still has time on it."

"Sure mom," I said, tucking the phone into my pocket. "Where will you be staying?" I asked.

"Oh, in some nice hotel," mommy smiled. "Buckle up," she said and drove off when I did.

I knew going to grandma's would be a lot of fun. My body automatically slumped down in the seat as we drove by where the Mozis lived. I held my breath while we passed all the officers standing around. My mother nodded driving by. Her cell phone rang.

"Hey Ramirez. I'm all right. You're going on vacation? Oh, I'm jealous. I'm taking Shareef to mommy. You have fun, Ramirez. I'll see you when you get back."

It was early evening when we reached grandma's home in the Bronx. They were expecting us, and there was pizza and sodas.

"Wash your hands and come and eat," grandma greeted.

There were hugs and kisses all around. My mother's two sisters and their children were there. It seemed like a family reunion.

While the adults sat around talking, my cousins and I chomped down slice after slice. Then we washed it all down with soda. We played video games like it was a weekend. Then hours later, the adults were finished with their powwow.

"Shareef, say good night to mommy," my mother said.

I walked over to where she was standing with her arms outstretched, gave her a hug, kissed her and whispered in her ear.

"I love you, mom."

"Shareef, please remember to brush your teeth before

going to sleep. Get some rest and don't you give grandma a hard time," she said, squeezing my hand, and kissing my cheek.

"Okay mommy," I said.

I felt sadness watching the door shut. Suddenly she was gone. Although grandma, my cousin and aunt remained, I felt lonely.

"All right Shareef, go on and get ready for bed," grandma said.

"I gotta brush my teeth before I go to bed."

I saw my cousin and his mother disappearing into the bathroom and waited. When they were out, I went in and stared into the darkened mirror. The doorbell sounded and I heard my aunt rushing to the door.

"Who is it?" she asked. "Is that you, Rita?"

I heard the door being unlocked. Thinking that my mother had somehow changed her mind, I was about to open the bathroom door. My body froze when my aunt shrieked. The frightening noise shattered the silence and all my senses.

My breath stopped when the sound of gunshots from an automatic weapon exploded in the living room. Terrified, I fell to the floor and crawled into a corner.

They moved so quickly I didn't have time to shut the

bathroom door completely. Through the opening, I had seen gunshots dropping Aunt Lila in a bloody heap. Feet went by the bathroom briskly.

"Check all the rooms quickly!" One of them loudly hissed.

The door of my grandmother's rooms slammed hard against the wall when a boot came in contact with it.

"Get out of my room, murderers!"

My grandmother's scream was followed by a burst of gunshots. The sound of her body falling and her inaudible mumbling came after. Then there was silence.

I heard their footsteps systematically going through the apartment, checking all the bedrooms. Suddenly there was a spine-chilling scream coming from my cousin's room.

"Shut that damn kid up!" someone screamed.

"But he's only a kid," another replied.

"Okay, I'll do it."

There was more gunfire followed by another deadly silence. I crouched in the dark underneath the sink. My knees and teeth were rattling loudly, as the footsteps got closer and closer. The door to the bathroom was suddenly kicked in.

"Who's in here?"

I held my breath, shut my eyes and whispered a silent prayer. It seemed forever before the shoes moved away. I didn't want to look up at the face, but from my angle it wasn't difficult to see him. Crouching deeper into the darkness of my space, I shuddered when I heard them speaking.

"I think that's it."

"Ah... That cop ain't nowhere here."

"Well she'll definitely know what happens to anyone who snitches," one of them said with a chuckle.

They stood around for what seemed like an eternity, then I heard them walking out. I stayed low and didn't move long after the door had been slammed. Horrified, I waited for a long time. Cautious and slow, I made my way out. I felt nauseous when I saw blood all over the apartment.

Too scared, I couldn't look directly at my aunt. She wasn't moving and I knew from the pool of blood leaking out of her that she was probably dead. Nervously I crept to my cousin's room. I couldn't identify his body immediately. It looked like he was asleep on the floor until I saw all the blood on the other side of him.

"Grandma, grandma!" I yelled, shaking like a leaf in a strong wind.

I waited outside her door at the threshold, not daring to enter. I knocked loudly, but there was no response. I was too afraid to peek past the doorway. My mouth dropped open and I suddenly felt faint.

CHAPTER 15

Fear overwhelmed me. My breathing came in gasps. I rushed to the phone and dialed my mother's cell phone number. My mouth was dry by the time she picked up.

"Mommy, they kill grandma, they kill grandma, Aunt Lila and Tito! Mommy, mommy, they were all killed!" I blurted. "Yes, I'm sure. Three men came in through the door. They were wearing police uniforms, mommy."

She was saying a whole lot of things but I couldn't

understand anything. It was just sound to me.

"Everyone…" I said looking around. "I can't move, mommy. I'll wait for you."

Fear gripped me. Carnage was everywhere. The blood and gunpowder mix made me want to vomit. I understood enough to know my mother was on her way, and I put the phone down.

It took her forever but eventually my mother arrived. Her face was blank and focused, her badge around her neck. Then the cavalry arrived, a sea of blue. I vomited the moment they walked inside.

An officer came racing through and gasped when he saw the bodies. "What the hell happened here?" Mother was running through the door checking the rooms. I heard her blood-curdling scream when she saw her mother.

"Oh my God…! Mommy…!"

Time seemed to stand still. Nothing moved. My mother was dragged away shaking her head and screaming. I felt the horror of the whole thing in that single moment. The pain that clouded my mother's face will always stay imprinted on my brain. She sat in the middle of the floor. Paramedics rushed to her side. I bawled when I saw how soiled my mother was from the blood of her family. I ran to her. She closed her eyes and cried.

Our worst nightmare had exploded right here in my grandma's apartment. I tried to fathom, but just couldn't. My head whirled as I saw my mother's twisted face, the look on the face of the police and paramedics streaming around the place.

"Are you alright?" the paramedic asked. "I mean were you shot, or hurt in any way?" he asked.

My father was trying to get through the throng of police officers and crime scene personnel that had descended.

"That's my boy," he yelled at an officer.

"Let him through," Mother said.

He came over and hugged us both. We were taken outside walking in each other's embrace. For a second, being with my dad felt right. Mom, dad and I huddled together. Mother sobbed softly against his shoulders.

I shook my head. One by one the bodies were being carried out in black body bags. Tears were streaming down my mother's face. She hugged me tightly and released me when an officer gently tugged on her arm.

"Rita… Officer Sanchez. We need your permission to talk to your son."

My mother turned and looked at me. I held on to my parents tighter. Mother loosened my grip.

"Are you gonna be able to talk to the officers, Shareef?" she asked.

Still holding my dad's hand, I moved closer to her.

"Rita, Shareef is too scared to be talking…"

"Please, officer escort this man out," she said turning to an officer.

"All right sir, you've got to go."

"But Rita," dad protested.

"Calm down," the officer said, grabbing hold of his arm, and pulling him away.

"All right, all right, I'm going," dad said as he was being led away. Mother turned her attention to me.

"Just tell them what you saw," she said.

I looked at the officers for a minute and shook my head.

"What's the problem, Shareef? Would you prefer if I go with you?"

I nodded.

"Good, I will," she said, holding my hand.

I sat in the car still feeling nauseous. My mother sat on

one side and a detective on the other.

"I am Detective Jackson. I'm going to ask you about the shooting, alright Shareef? Can you remember how it all started?"

I stared at him and felt terrible pain in my stomach. It felt like my stomach was in a knot. My mouth went dry and I wanted to urinate.

"Are you alright, Shareef?" my mother asked.

Before I could give a reply I was vomiting all over the detective's car. He made a face getting out of the way. My mother searched her pocketbook and gave me a pack of napkins. Then she helped to scrub my face and hands. She wiped frantically here and there as best she could, then went outside and spoke to the officer. Minutes later, she returned and opened the door of the car.

"Shareef, you can tell me what you saw, I'll write the statement and you can sign it. That's what the detective said."

I nodded.

Mother sat in the car with a pen and pad ready.

"Now all you gotta do is tell me what happened," she said. Her voice was clear and her confidence reassured me.

For a few minutes I said nothing. I looked out the window seeing the police rushing in and out taking notes. Everyone seemed to have a walkie-talkie.

"What is it, Shareef?"

"Mom," I said after a while. "They were all wearing uniforms."

"What kind of uniforms?"

I hesitated before uttering the words, "Police uniforms…"

"Shareef, are you sure? My whole family was just killed. Please, try to be clear…"

"Mom, I mean when the doorbell rang, the men were in police uniforms."

"I swear to God, Shareef. This better not be more of your lies!"

I nodded.

"Now, Shareef, you're not just saying this because you've been acting…"

"Mom, I saw them. There were three men. They rang the doorbell and Aunt Lila went to answer the door. She asked if it was you, then I don't know what they said, but she let them inside. Then they started shooting everyone."

"What do you mean they started shooting everyone?"

"First they shot Aunt Lila then they went after grandma. She tried to keep them out of her room but they were firing guns and she couldn't stop them."

"Did you see any of their faces or, what they looked like?"

"They had masks pulled down over their faces too quickly for me to see them."

"And you're sure they were wearing police uniforms?"

"Yeah mommy, I swear they were."

My mother stared at me. The look of disbelief was wrinkled on her face even though she sounded as if she wanted to believe me. She asked me to recount what happened without retelling it and I tried my best to comply. When I was finished, she continued asking more questions.

"What about badges? Could you see any badges?"

I thought about it for a minute and shook my head. "You're sure about this, Shareef?" I nodded again.

She opened the door of the car and walked quickly over to the officer. Mother and the detective raced back to me.

"Are you sure they were police officers?" he asked.

"Please talk to us," mother pleaded.

"Yes they were three men and they were all dressed in police uniforms," I answered.

I felt an explosion coming; the nausea was a warning I

couldn't ignore. I vomited again and again.

"Not that I don't believe your son, but I'll double check and see if there were any officers responding to calls anywhere in this vicinity. Maybe we can round up a few eyewitnesses to collaborate your son's story."

The hush-hush jibber-jabber of police-talk between my mother and the detective continued. They both cast pitying glances at me. Then both headed back closer. My mother was looking at me as if I'd done something wrong.

"Here Shareef, take this," she said.

I took the moistened napkin and wiped my face. My sticky hands, I saved for last. I watched them watching my every move. Finally the detective spoke.

"Shareef, we're gonna have to verify your story. Is there anything else that you saw and didn't tell us?"

I shook my head. I knew she did not believe me and was just too weak to argue with me.

"If you remember anything else, anything at all, you can call me, okay, Shareef?" The detective turned to my mother and continued. "Get in touch with me immediately if he says anything." He walked away with the information written down and signed by me.

"Shareef," mother said with tears in her eyes. "Are you feeling any better?"

I was about to answer when another officer approached us.

"We'll have round the clock guards at two different hotels. You and your family will occupy one and a team of decoys, the other," he said when he reached us.

A group of detectives quickly escorted my mother and me to a waiting car. Four detectives stood guard while mother and I got inside. The car settled into second place in a convoy of three cars. The questions followed.

"I heard your boy had a hard time back there. Does he need a doctor?" the sergeant asked.

"Under the circumstances, Sergeant, I would say that's a good idea," My mother answered hugging me.

"So kid I heard you were there when those, ah, killers came in?"

I had my eyes fixed on the traffic slipping by. Lights flashing and the loud siren announced our arrival. It was overwhelming to me. Pedestrians on the sidewalk stopped to stare at us. I could hear the detective still jawing.

"Is he alright? He doesn't look too well."

My mother looked down on me. She could feel my sweaty palm inside her hand. I was nervous but I was getting strength from her.

CHAPTER 16

They walked around us. Our escorts were constantly checking behind and in front, signal here and there. Their every move seemed precise and planned. In no time, we had changed clothes and walked into the elevator dressed in clown costumes. We walked into the hotel room and I came face to face with my stepfather. He looked ragged and disheveled like he had aged twice since the last time I saw him.

"Hey, Shareef," he jumped from the bed and greeted. We

hugged briefly. Then he embraced mother. "I'm so sorry about what happened," he said somberly.

"It's not your fault," mother said hugging him. "Why haven't you shaven?"

"Apparently, someone ordered a twenty-four hour suicide watch on me. I was complaining about not letting me go with too much. Everything that comes in has to be thoroughly checked."

"Now who would do something like that? I mean I can't imagine," mother said. She was deep in thoughts when the doorbell rang. It was the doctor. He came carrying a bag and frowned when he glanced at me. It was the same therapist who had examined me previously.

"Oh my," he said walking over to where I stood very nervous. "It's, ah, Shareef." He reached out and grabbed my hand. "Go ahead and remove your shirt, I'll make some checks. What you witnessed was brutal, I know. Try to relax for now," he said.

I cooperated with his examinations. In the end, he offered medication.

"This will help him sleep," he explained, handing my mother a bottle of pills. She examined it carefully, then looked at my stepfather and finally at me.

"Are you sure this will not have any serious side effects?" she asked.

"Minimal," he said packing his bags. "You may put your shirt back on," he instructed as he headed to the door. "I'll see you in my office at ten in the morning."

He was almost out the door, when mother caught up to him and said.

"Doctor, we've got to be in court tomorrow."

"As far as I know, only one parent will be needed in court tomorrow. The other person who is free can bring the child to my office at ten o'clock in the morning. Good night, Officer."

My mother slammed the door and walked over to where my stepfather and I were.

"What was that all about?" he asked.

"Shareef had seen him a couple days ago, and he wants to do a follow-up tomorrow. He wants to run more tests."

"What kind of tests?" My stepfather asked.

"He feels that Shareef is internalizing what's going on around him and that's causing him to exhibit an intense fear of the police. The upset stomach is another reaction from the fear. The therapist said that Shareef told him that a cop from my precinct was one of the killers. The therapist thinks Shareef is transferring all bad things to men in uniform all because he was arrested and was scared by the officers. I really don't know what else to do…" her voice trailed.

"Honey, I had no idea. With the situation with me, and now your mother being—"

"Please, do not bring that up. I can't bear this. I've got to bury my…"

My stepfather shushed her and my mother cried in his arms. I walked over and hugged her. Teary-eyed she looked down at me.

"Are you sure the men who came knocking on grandma's door were police officers, Shareef?" she asked.

I stared at her as I thought about the question for a beat too long.

"Shareef, tell me, the men who murdered your grandma, your aunt and cousin were police?" my stepfather asked with a hint of disbelief on his tongue.

"Don't badger the boy. That's what he saw," my mother countered.

"Is that what happened, Shareef? Tell me what happened," my stepfather ordered. I remained quiet.

"Stanley, please do not put my son through that again."

"Hell, I'm married to you. That makes him my son too."

"Yes, even so, that doesn't make it open season."

"Just what're you trying to say here?"

"You best be thinking what you're going to be telling that grand jury tomorrow morning. I'll come and see for myself as soon as the therapist is through examining Shareef," my mother said.

My stepfather backed off from his questions. I felt somewhat better for the moment.

"Shareef, it's bedtime," mother said.

I did not take long to fall asleep, but not before thinking about seeing the therapist in the morning.

———————

I awoke the next morning and was surprised by my surroundings. Yawning while surveying, I saw my stepfather sitting on the sofa. He was dressed, drinking coffee and watching the news. The segment showed everything that happened the night before at my grandmother's apartment. The reporter called it a massacre. Waking up to the bad news only served to alarm me further. I started to scrutinize the people around me.

My mother had an intense look of disgust on her face. My stepfather seemed like he was cramping. I was reminded that the horrific incident last night was not a nightmare. It had really happened. My grandmother, cousin and aunt had been executed right in front of my eyes.

I continued to watch the television and noticed that the news reporter had left out my name but talked about an eyewitness. There was no mention of killers wearing police uniforms. I guessed no one believed me.

"Shareef, get to the bathroom and get dressed."

"Okay mom."

"Are the make-up people from the feds on their way yet?" she asked my stepfather.

"It's the feds, so they don't say when they're coming, they just show up. But I think that they'll be here any minute, sweetheart," he said.

The mood was tense and I could see the worried look on my mother's face when I came out of the bathroom. Two people dressed in lab coats flanked my stepfather. They must be make-up, I thought. The whole scene reminded me of a bad thriller.

What was going to happen next? After my grandmother's killing, who knew?

The police were preparing for the worst. They sent a four-man escort team for my stepfather. Later two officers returned to escort us using another exit.

Morning traffic was light as we headed downstairs and to the cars. Two officers followed the car. Our driver was a police officer and I immediately felt nauseous.

"Motion sickness," my mother said.

I held my head out the window and barfed. We went directly into the therapist office. Mother sat outside and I went inside with him.

"Good morning, Shareef. How're you feeling?" he asked in a chirpy voice.

I wanted to tell him about the nightmare I was living, but I knew that might get me officially classified as cuckoo.

"Good morning, doctor," I answered.

"Okay, Shareef, I want you to talk freely about everything you're feeling…" his words drifted through the air.

Mentally, I crawled back under the sink, holding my breath and thinking that there was something creepy about this man. At the end of the session, he would prescribe more medication. I did everything to block out the maniac sitting across from me.

Later we walked out together. He was beaming after the session.

"I think we've made great progress," he announced when my mother walked over.

"I'm glad. Really, I'm happy. Doctor, can we wrap this up? I'd like to get over to the court. You know, traffic."

"Yes, sure, we're going to increase his meds and see how he does. Then from there we'll lower the concentration."

"Okay, but why are you increasing the dosage?"

"I'm afraid that's the only way we can help your son. He has a chemical imbalance and what the concentrated form does is balance him out so to speak," he said, and slapped me on the back.

His slight shove, propelled me forward and I found myself hugging my mother. She had a sympathetic smile.

"Shareef has been through a lot. Thank you doctor for all your help," my mother said as we readied to leave.

"You're most welcome and here's another bottle. Please make sure you give him as directed. Any questions, you've got my number."

Mother grabbed the bottle and put it in her purse. She hauled me to the elevator and we boarded. She was dialing on her cell phone when we got off. Downstairs, we waited for the escort to bring the car around.

"I don't like coming to that doctor, he bugs me out," I said as I watched the car slowly moving closer and closer.

Mother was still on the phone. She turned, looked at me and said, "What did you say, Shareef?"

I was preoccupied with the approaching car. I grabbed at mother and pointed.

"Mommy, look. That's not the same car!" I screamed.

She looked just in time to see the car windows coming down and gunshots erupting.

"Get down!" Mother shouted, pushing me to the ground and diving on top of me.

She pushed me behind another car as gunshots were fired at us. Safely concealed behind an automobile, my mother pulled out her gun and returned fire. I felt adrenaline rushing through me as shells flew.

"Stay down, Shareef!" she ordered.

On her hands and knees, she scurried to the front of the car and got a jump on the bad guys. Mother let loose with a barrage of gunfire. Then there was silence. She gave me the thumbs up signal, crept close to the other car and started a body count.

"They're all dead," she said into her phone, returning to where I was. "Okay, I'll stay here until you send a team out here. Make it quick I wanted to be in court."

Mother then closed the cell phone and hurried to where I was. She wasn't smiling when she asked, "Are you alright, Shareef?"

I was completely overwhelmed by the way my mother had handled herself. It was a revealing performance. I felt a rush of excitement. I had to hug her.

"I'm alright," I said, breathing hard. I had just witnessed something shocking but spectacular. "I guess this is one of the times that you've got to fight back."

CHAPTER 17

All of a sudden it happened. With my mother still on her cell phone, there were police all over the place. In a matter of minutes, I went from elation to nausea. Mother seemed content giving statements and speaking with the officers. I cuddled next to her and only felt better when she turned to me and said.

"Let's go."

We walked with a group of officers to a car and sped off. Lights and sirens blared as we made our way to the courthouse.

"I can't believe me and my son's lives were in danger because we happened to stop at a Dunkin Donuts. That's a joke," my mother complained.

Detectives were in cars in front and behind us. Our driver was a detective. I felt that crawling in my stomach and tried to watch the road. We arrived at the courthouse and the same four detectives signaled for us to walk in. Inside, I sat nervously next to mother and waited.

"Are you all right?" she asked me.

I nodded, but knew I wasn't. I was trying desperately to be brave. Back there in the streets, my mother had shown so much bravery; I just couldn't be weak. All around us there were officers in uniform walking back and forth. Detectives seemed to swarm like the cavalry. Some stopped to speak with mother, while others just stared. I was petrified, and just sat quietly. One of the officers walked over briskly. He gave mother a friendly hug.

"Hey Ramirez, how are you?" my mother greeted the man.

"Hi Rita, I came as soon as heard you were in here."

"I'm happy to see you. Oh, you remember my son, Shareef."

"Shareef, nice to meet you."

"Hi," I said, trying not to be seen.

He was wearing sunglasses and pulled them down to wave at me. I could see the ring. I could see right through him.

"Shareef, you remember my partner, Officer Ramirez."

"Ah, you know you can call me Charlie," the officer smiled and waved. "I'm really sorry about your family. that must've been really horrible. I didn't know about anything until a couple hours ago."

"Right, you were out on vacation."

"It must be going rough, huh?"

"I'm getting by. I guess I'll feel different Friday at the funeral."

"That's two days from now. I'm there."

"Thanks Ramirez."

"C'mon, we're partners, right?" They hugged.

"You're still a sweetheart."

"So, what's going on…" they both started asking the same question at the same time.

"Go ahead," he said.

"How did your family enjoy Disneyworld?"

"It was beautiful. Everyone had fun."

"What were you about to say, Ramirez?"

"Oh, um, how was it going with the grand jury?" the officer asked.

"They're still taking depositions. I don't think he's testified yet. I came too late to see before he went inside."

"You are always on time."

"I guess it had to do with a certain hit."

"Yeah, really—what're you talking about?"

"Boy, you've been really out on vacation, huh?

"Rita, you know…"

"Save it. I thought you knew what happened."

"I arrived this morning at LaGuardia, went home and came right here."

"Earlier this morning after I took Shareef for his appointment a car came around and took potshots at me and my son."

"Are you serious? I didn't hear anything about it."

"It happened about an hour ago in broad daylight."

"Really…? No one said anything to me," Ramirez said. He was wide-eyed with surprise.

"Yes, you were still in vacation mode. You were out the loop."

"All right, you don't have to rub it in."

"I'm saying that when you're on these vacations of yours…"

"C'mon, Rita something goes on with my partner, I wouldn't take it lightly. Especially an attempt on her life. Tell me how many were there?"

"It was the driver and one other. I shot them both."

"That'll show them who they can't mess with."

"I think whoever was trying to kill us—it's more than likely the same people who killed the Mozis. You know… my neighbors and their daughter?"

"Yeah, I remember the incident. They were gunned down in their driveway, right?"

"Those killers haven't been caught."

"I know a friend who's working on it. He told me they've got nothing except motive, shells and the bodies." Ramirez was glancing around as she spoke.

"Everything started happening after Mozi was set to testify."

"Yes, the killers are probably the same ones who killed… Mom, Lila and Tito." My mother looked away.

"That makes sense. The news made it seem as if it

was some type of accident. Now they're coming after you and Shareef."

"It doesn't add up to anything but hits. My mother's place was not ransacked. Nothing was stolen."

"I get your drift. As soon as they found out your husband was gonna cooperate they targeted your family also."

"It's more like the minute he was scheduled to testify to the grand jury. That same evening, the hit was made at my mother's. The attempt to kill me and my son this morning and all the other hits are related."

"There's no mention of that in the papers."

"The newspaper made it appear like the killers were looking for another apartment. My mother wasn't involved. She doesn't owe anyone anything. Why was she targeted? Whoever did it is trying to prevent my husband from testifying. They know we're his immediate family. So they're coming after us to get to him."

"Hmm, you can never believe the newspapers, can you?" Ramirez said, scratching his head. "It's sensationalism. Their theory just distorts the facts. It's an advantage to the bad guys. They could hide under the reporter's error."

"The fact is no one knew about him cooperating. No one,

that is except the prosecutors and detectives," Mother said.

"Hmm… You knew?" Ramirez asked, looking intensely at Mother.

"Yeah, but I certainly wasn't going to run out and tell anyone. Not even my own mother. To make matters worse, Shareef—the only eyewitness to any of the murders—said the killers were wearing police uniforms. Now, you know they called the doctor uh…the therapist who's been seeing my son."

"I know. What happened?"

"They are trying to dismiss it," mother said. Her voice sounded annoyed.

"Based on what?" Ramirez asked, looking confused.

"The lead detective is alleging my son's mental capacity is in question and he doubts whether it was worth the manpower…" Mother's voice trailed.

She glanced back at me, tugged on the arm of Ramirez and they walked a few feet out of my earshot.

A few minutes later, they walked back. I could tell that Ramirez was making every attempt not to stare at me. Maybe they all thought I was going crazy.

"I was out of the loop. Now I'm back. Nobody will be taking potshots anymore. Right, Shareef?" he smiled at me.

"Thanks partner. I know you've got my back," Mother said as she patted him.

"That's how it's supposed to be, right?" Ramirez turned and hugged her.

"You've got that right," mother responded triumphantly.

"Why don't we run down to the station house and do that paperwork?"

"I want to be here when he's through. I can't afford anything else to go wrong with my family."

"I understand. Listen, I'm going to the station house anything you want me to tell the sergeant?" Ramirez asked.

"No, I just got off the phone with him. I'll be allowed to do the paperwork in the morning."

"Rita, I'll catch up to you later. Remember now, partner, you don't have to go through this alone."

Ramirez kissed my mother's cheek, then slapped my hand and walked out of the court. Mother and I were left still waiting.

CHAPTER 18

That evening, my mother, stepfather and I returned to the hotel. They tried to keep it down, but I could feel the tension in the air.

"I can't believe those murderers did what they did!" My stepfather shouted, throwing the newspaper across the room. "Coming at you and Shareef, it's just not right!"

"The only thing that's right is for you to cooperate with the prosecutors. Then all this can somehow come to an end," mother said.

She threw a cautionary glance at me sitting in front of the television. I was pretending my thoughts were buried in the sitcom. Our lives had become so dramatic that everywhere we went there were armed officers present.

"Yeah, yeah just cooperate. 'Just cooperate with the DA,' you told Mozi and you see what resulted. His family buried him, his wife and his only child a week ago. You actually think that they're going to let this end the way you want it to go?"

"No I don't, but I'm prepared to stay on the side of the law. It's the only way I know."

"That's easy for you to say, you haven't—"

"Don't tell me what I haven't done," mother said. Then she looked at me. "Go to your room, Shareef," she ordered.

"My room…? Mommy we're in a hotel," I reminded her.

"I don't care. You know what I mean. Go in the bedroom and don't give me any more lip."

"But mommy, I didn't do anything," I countered.

"Shareef, if you don't get your butt inside that room right now, I'll come over there and you won't like it."

"It's not my fault that this is happening," I said, looking defiantly at my mother.

I ran in the bedroom when I saw her heading toward me. She followed me and slammed the door so hard it flew back open. She walked away leaving the door halfway opened. They were shouting loud enough and I didn't have to do a lot to hear most of their conversation.

"This was no fault of mine or my mother. But she was killed along with my sister and her son. Who have you lost? Your friend, Mr. Mozi? Remember he was the one who got you in all this mess. He is the one, if anyone, who should've suffered all the loss. My mother and sister were not involved—or her son. This morning, Shareef and I easily could've been murdered. My son was seconds away from his death through no fault of his. Did I run and tell you that it was your fault? No I didn't. Now you're telling me about reneging on the deal with the DA."

"Rita, I'm not saying I'm not going to cooperate. All I'm saying is that it is a difficult situation."

"Difficult my ass…! You should've thought it all out clearly before you went and did what you did. Everyday it's something new. First, you had no idea of what was going on. You were involved with smuggling drugs into the country. You were a mule for these criminals, and it is your actions that spelled doom for my mother. She did nothing. Nothing! And was executed because of your irrational actions."

There was a continuous knocking at the door. The doorbell sounded. Mother opened the door and an officer stepped inside.

"Is everything alright in here?"

"Yes," mother responded curtly.

"I heard the ruckus and just wanted to make sure," the officer said, an inquisitive grin plastered on his face.

"We're just having a discussion. Were we too loud for you?"

"Well I could hear all that you guys were saying and…"

"We'll keep it down, thank you, officer."

"Okay, I'll be right outside," the officer said.

"How many of you are on duty?"

"There are two of us and we're right outside."

"Thank you officer, we'll keep it down," mother said.

She walked back to where my stepfather was sitting after the officer walked out. There was calmness in her voice but her expression registered anger.

"Whatever happened doesn't matter. We're all in it now," she said as the telephone rang. "Yes," she said answering it. "Ramirez, what's up? Yes, we're all safe here in the hotel. Thanks for checking in. Yes, I'll be at work in the morning. Huh-uh, yes…"

She stayed on for a few more seconds then hung up.

"Who was that?" my stepfather asked.

"That was my patrol partner, Carlos Ramirez. I know good people. You want to run with the bad guys and that's what caused all these problems."

"Do you think my testimony will correct all the wrong I've done?"

"I think the least that can happen is your testimony will help send the criminals to jail."

"What about you and me, our family and life together?"

"I don't know what's in store for you and I. Only time will tell…"

"I mean is there any way for us to get back to where we were?"

"I don't know, Stanley. I really don't know."

"It's a high cost to pay for the price of justice."

"Tell me about it."

After that exchange, their voices went silent. All I heard was the news on the television. Her cell phone rang loudly.

"Lenny, I told you not to call me unless…" her voce trailed.

I kept my ears perked, but after several minutes, I too let it go. I fell asleep.

CHAPTER 19

A loud explosion rocked the building and awoke me. I jumped out of bed and ran to where my mother was. I met her in the midst of the rubble and ash in the hotel room. The sprinkler system was going at full blast and everything was wet.

"Shareef, Shareef, are you alright?" she asked.

"Yes, I am—"

I was coughing and couldn't see very clearly. Mother

had her gun in hand and cautiously she went to what was left of the door. Before she could open it, gunshots were coming at her. She dropped to the floor and crawled back over to where I was.

"Are you alright, son?"

"Yes, mother."

"Stay down," she said.

"Mom, what's going on? Are they trying to kill us?"

I wanted to ask more questions but she was running to the bathroom. My stepfather was inside.

"Open the door! Stanley, open the door now! It's Rita!" She shouted as a few more shots came at us.

The door to the bathroom swung open and my stepfather came out looking scared. He immediately got behind mother when another volley of shots came at us. Mother waited for a moment then she ran to the bedroom, grabbed her cell phone and dialed.

"Ramirez, get your ass over to the hotel right now, buddy. Bring backup—we're under attack," she said and hung up.

There were more barrages of gunfire. Mother never returned fire but kept her gun in hand ready.

"I think they're sweeping the area," she said.

Another burst of gunfire and then someone kicked the

hotel door down. Mother threw me to the ground and let off shot after shot. She kept firing until all that could be heard was the sound of bullets ricocheting off walls. Then there was a grunt.

"Ooh ugh…"

A few seconds later, the peaceful sound of the water sprinkler and the beat of my heart racing were all that was left going. I'm alive, I thought. Looking around, I could see that the white of my stepfather's eyes were visible. He was perspiring like crazy, and he appeared to be paralyzed by his fear.

"Shareef, where's your mother?" he whispered.

I glanced at him again, blinking hard to see if he was injured. Realizing that he was afraid and incapable of moving, I relaxed my stare. The confirmation that he was all right didn't stop my heart from palpitating. I felt like I was about to pass out and tried to calm myself. I had to be fearless for Mother. Where was she? I anxiously glanced around the room, straining my eyes trying to find her.

My breath was swept away when I heard footsteps and miraculously she appeared at the entrance of the doorway. Her gun was visible in her hand. She grabbed her cell phone and dialed.

"Two officers down… Maybe killed. There are also two

other unidentified bodies… I am alright," she said and hung up.

Mother hugged me close and stared at my stepfather as if he was pariah.

"Rita, oh Rita, what've I done? I can't go down for this," he cried.

I realized his was the voice I heard in the house that night! It was his familiar voice I heard saying, "I can't go down for this."

A few more minutes of silence and the place was teeming with police officers. There were news people and cameras everywhere snapping pictures of this and that. Inquires came from all angles. The police and reporters were having a field day. Then the firefighters and paramedics rushed the scene.

Mother remained calm throughout the ordeal. She answered questions with aplomb, despite the circumstances. My mother already did not want to believe what I told her about the detectives and she was not going to listen. My stepfather seemed flustered and agitated. He kept yelling at the reporters.

"Get your cameras out of my face or I'll break them!" he warned.

It was easy to tell that he didn't want to be here. It wasn't my kind of wakeup either, so leaving my stepfather cursing at everyone. I stuck like glue to my mother.

I remembered the question he had asked mother last night. It had to do with whether or not things would ever get back to normal. He was a murderer, a drug dealer and a coward—and I was the only one who knew the truth.

Ramirez was by my mother's side as she fielded queries from the lead detectives working on my grandma's killing. There were uniformed and civilian-attired personnel sitting around us. I felt queasy, but safe by mother's side.

"What were they wearing? How many were there? Were you able to get a good look at any of them?"

Mother answered and in an equally precise manner. She was confident and there were no glitches in her explanation. My stepfather was flustered and became agitated sitting around waiting for his interrogation.

When the questions were aimed at him, my stepfather went into a rage.

"What do I care what uniforms they were wearing? All I know is they were trying to kill my family and me. Your guards let us down. How can I feel safe?"

Mother sat with members of the police from her precinct methodically breaking each step of the assault down. She pulled

Ramirez aside.

"The chief's been asking who knew where we were," she said. Then paused. "You were the only one who knew we had switched hotels."

"I was?"

"Yes, you were. What did you do? You didn't compromise security, now did you, Charlie?"

"Rita, we're partners I wouldn't do anything like that. I called to see how you were doing then I hung up and went to have some drinks."

"You went drinking with one of your floozies? You could have said something to tip someone off."

"Rita, you're wrong on that point. I went out with the boys from the task force, had a few drinks, then I went home to sleep."

"Oh sure, new friends, huh…? And that's it?"

"Yes Rita, that's it."

"I wonder who could've let the location slip out."

"Why do you think that…?"

"Charlie, can't you see, if nobody else knew, then it had to be an inside job."

"An inside job, how can that be? Are you sure, Rita?"

"C'mon, I really can't be sure, unless I know for sure."

"Damn right. Think maybe there was someone else who knew your whereabouts."

"You couldn't be more right. I'm starting to feel some type of cover-up."

"As soon as we left the therapist's office, an attempt was made. How could anyone else know I was taking my son to the…"

She looked at Ramirez. He looked at her.

"Someone in the department has a copy of my itinerary."

"What about his father?"

"You mean Lenny?" she asked.

"I mean you never know, Rita. He might be doing this for revenge. He doesn't particularly like you at this time."

"I've know Lenny since we were teens. He'll try kicking my ass, but he won't shoot at me, especially not while I'm with his son."

"Whoever is doing it definitely has you targeted to be murdered."

"Yeah, my son and I," mother said, pausing to look at me. I could tell her mind was on overdrive. "I'm going to take every possible precaution from now on," she turned to Ramirez and continued.

"That's a good idea," he said hugging her. "And limit the people you disclose your location to," Ramirez said, kissing her cheek. He waved and walked away.

Immediately queasiness overcame me. I wanted to vomit and walked to my mother.

"Mommy, I've gotta go."

I tugged on her sleeve and she gave me the 'I'm too busy' look. This only made me pull harder and before I knew it she was rushing off with me. She took me to another room.

"Mommy, mommy I know who was in the uniform at grandma's," I said urgently.

"Shareef, what're you trying to say?" she asked, gazing with annoyance at me.

"It was one of the officers that was with Charlie at the restaurant."

"Shareef, you cannot just go around pointing your fingers at people when you feel like it, accusing everyone. First, you told me it was the officer from the precinct, then now it's Ramirez's partner. The doctor is gonna help you alright."

She was frustrated walking away.

"But mommy," I said.

"Shareef, clean yourself before coming out."

CHAPTER 20

The next few days I didn't attend school as a precautionary measure, taken by mother. It was good for me. I needed the break from all the attention. Mother kept me close to her but at the same time remained emotionally distant. She was still in denial about everything I told her. Under the cover of extreme privacy, we ate and slept in the hotel, changing rooms each night. Security was tight.

Friday morning rolled around and we prepared to attend the funeral of my three relatives. It was a tough morning for my mother but she was determined to see us through this. My stepfather was still whining. On the day she had to see my grandmother, aunt and cousin put in the ground, he was agitated and anxious.

"I can't wait for this circus to be over." He complained as he dressed.

"It will. On Monday, you tell the grand jury all you know and that'll be all."

"How can you be sure I'll even live to see Monday, Rita?"

"Have faith, Stanley," mother continued while fixing his tie. "I think we're all ready," mother said, turning and giving me the once-over glance. "All right, let's go."

Four detectives appeared on cue and opened the door. They escorted us to the elevator. In the lobby, there were more detectives and police cars. Sirens blared and a convoy of cars proceeded to the church.

From the streets all the way inside there were officers in uniform and detectives. I sat in awe next to mother and listened to the preacher. There were a lot of speeches from people who didn't belong to the family. I think I heard all the politicians and everyone else running for city office. The killing had drawn local political support and there was a huge turnout. News reporters were sitting outside hours later when we came out.

Dad was there at the cemetery. Dressed in a black suit, he looked fresh and clean. He nodded and walked over to me.

"How're you doing, Shareef?"

He bent down and hugged me. There was no smell of liquor.

"I'm all right, dad. How're you doing?"

"Fine Shareef. You've been looking after mom?"

"Sure dad," I answered as mother and my stepfather came by.

The men shook hands cordially, and mother gave my dad a hug.

"Hello Lenny," she said.

"Rita, I'm sorry about your loss. Can we talk privately for a sec?" Dad said.

"I doubt that with all these officers around," mother said, pulling him a few steps away. "I want to talk to you and I've got to have your absolute trust," she said.

They walked away and spoke for a minute before

Ramirez joined.

"Shareef," he said, reaching out to shake my hand.

"Hi," I barely said. I felt like a lump had developed in my throat.

"Stanley, I'd like to offer my condolences to you and Rita," Ramirez said as my mother rejoined us.

They stared at each other. It was clear now that Stanley was terrified of Ramirez. Dad tugged at my shoulder. I turned hoping not to hear what he was about to say.

"You're going to be staying with me until this whole thing blows over."

"No, I don't wanna go…" I started to say and ran to mother.

"It's okay, Shareef. I think it's a good idea. The bad guys want to kill us all. I've got to trust that your dad will take better care of you at this time."

"But mom…"

"Shareef, you've got to trust me. I'm your mother, right?"

"Yeah mommy, I'll listen."

With tears in my eyes, I hugged mother, waved at my stepfather and walked away with Dad. We left the funeral in Dad's car. He drove straight to his place and we went upstairs.

"I've got some leftover pizza from last night," he said, tossing his jacket on a crowded sofa.

My dad's place reminded me of my room. Everything was out of place. It seemed like he too was awaiting mommy's attention. She would have him working all day to clean up this mess. The television needed dusting, but it worked. Dad saw me trying to find the remote.

"I think it's underneath the cushion over by the lamp," he said pointing. I found it and began channel surfing. "I'm gonna warm these slices, do you care for any, son?"

"No dad," I answered.

Our lives had become crazy and he seemed really calm. Maybe I had inherited all my craziness from him. The microwave sounded and he joined me in front of the TV. Hearing him chomp on the pizza made me want to try one.

"Go ahead, get one if you feel like," he said, sitting down. "And get a napkin too. I don't want you dripping sauce all over the sofa."

I looked around the living room, broken lamp on the floor wondering about a drop of sauce. Dad was fun, but I decided right then that he was also a lunatic. The evening wore on with us watching television. Despite everything that happened I felt relaxed around dad. It was his swagger or that certain uncaring attitude that appeared to be confidence.

After a while both of us were nodding off. The doorbell rang followed by a knock. We both opened our eyes, looking incredulously at the door. Dad tiptoed to the door and looked out the peephole. He immediately came back found his cell phone and dialed.

"He's here," he said, and closed the cell phone. Dad lowered the volume on the television. "Who's there?" he asked.

"It's Ramirez," was the reply.

Dad shushed me and moved closer to the door.

"I don't know any Ramirez. You must have the wrong apartment."

"C'mon, you know me. I'm officer Ramirez—your ex's partner. Remember me?"

"Vaguely…"

"We can talk about this when I get inside. Open the door."

"No, I can't just let anyone up in my apartment."

Dad's words were cut by the sound of gunshots. Then the door was being stomped. It fell open. Dad grabbed a baseball bat but Ramirez walked in, gun raised accompanied by the two detectives who had interrogated me and beat dad up at the jail.

"Drop it!"

The bat fell from dad's hand slowly.

"All I want is the kid," he said, aiming the gun at dad. "I'll kill you if I have to, that's not my problem."

When he was sure dad wasn't about to make any moves, Ramirez still pointing the gun, walked past him. One of them tried to grab my arm but I ran.

"Remember me, kid? I'll put a cap in your legs then you won't run."

The other detectives grabbed me. For a second, Ramirez became distracted by my movement, and did not notice that dad had moved closer. Dad lunged at him and he tried to dodge but toppled backwards over the lamp. That was the advantage dad needed. The detectives released me to run to the aid of Ramirez. My dad was on top of Ramirez feeding him rights and lefts, just the way he had taught me. Proud excitement had me rooted to the spot.

"Get out of here, Shareef!"

I turned to run, but changed my mind and stayed. I just couldn't bring myself to leave Dad's side. The detectives tried holding him off to no avail. Dad kept hitting away. They were both big men and the fight was scary. Each second seemed like a lifetime.

A gunshot went off. The detective fired a shot into my father's abdomen to still his fist. Ramirez jumped to his feet. He stood up aimed his gun and was about to finish my dad off.

"Drop your gun, Ramirez!"

He looked up and saw mother standing in the doorway. The gun in her hand was aimed at him. The other detectives dropped their weapons.

Wobbled by dad's blows, he turned unsteadily and faced her. A sardonic smile creased Ramirez's lips. The realization that I was standing between him and mother hit him.

"Put down your gun, Charlie. Please don't make me do this," she pleaded.

For a beat it appeared as if Ramirez would comply. Suddenly he raised his gun. Mother was like a cat when she pounced, pushed me out of the way, and fired three times. The bullets ripped through Ramirez's body. He fell back against the littered sofa and blood oozed from his stomach. Mother rolled and immediately grabbed me.

"Are you all right?" she asked. She kept her guns pointed at the other detectives.

"Cuff yourselves!" She commanded, keeping control of

the scene.

They did as ordered. They knew what she was capable of after seeing what she did to their partner in crime. I nodded and she quickly raced to dad's side. Mother checked his pulse then ran to Ramirez. She was dialing on her cell phone when his hand fell limp.

"One dead, the other still breathing..." She closed the phone and surveyed the room. "We're gonna have to do some cleaning up around here." She hugged me.

"Shareef, I should have believed you. I'm sorry."

"It's all over now. Lolo's killers are where they belong. That was all I wanted."

"Then it is true. Stanley was really more involved than he let on."

"Yes mom. He was in the house that night that I snuck out. It was him and these detectives."

"I'm gonna call the DA and let them know that he should carry the full weight of the crimes. Did you keep the evidence you collected?"

"I did. I have been carrying it with me at all times in my backpack."

The tears rolled from her eyes. Once again, she was

wrong about the man she loved and once again, she would have to be alone. Minutes later, the cavalry arrived.

THE END

THiN LiNE

Our titles interlace action, crime, and the urban lifestyle depicting the harsh realities of life on the streets. Call it street literature, urban drama, we call it hip-hop literature. This exciting genre features fast-paced action, gritty ghetto realism, and social messages about the high price of the street life style.

DEAD AND STINKIN'
STEPHEN HEWETT

A GOOD DAY TO DIE
JAMES HENDRICKS

WHEN LOVE TURNS TO HATE
SHARRON DOYLE

IF IT AIN'T ONE THING IT'S ANOTHER
SHARRON DOYLE

WOMAN'S CRY
VANESSA MARTIR

BLACKOUT
JERRY LaMOTHE
ANTHONY WHYTE

HUSTLE HARD
BLAINE MARTIN

A BOOGIE DOWN STORY
KEISHA SEIGNIOUS

CRAVE ALL LOSE ALL
ERICK S GRAY

LOVE AND A GANGSTA
ERICK S GRAY

AMERICA'S SOUL
ERICK S GRAY   L

Mail us a List of the titles you would like include $14.95 per Title + shipping charges $3.95 for one book & $1.00 for each additional book. Make all checks payable to: Augustus Publishing 33 Indian Rd. NY, NY 10034

HARD WHITE
SHANNON HOLMES
ANTHONY WHYTE

STREET CHIC
ANTHONY WHYTE

BOOTY CALL *69
ERICK S GRAY

POWER OF THE P
JAMES HENDRICKS

STREETS OF NEW YORK VOL. 1
ERICK S GRAY, ANTHONY WHYTE
MARK ANTHONY, SHANNON HOLMES

STREETS OF NEW YORK VOL. 2
ERICK S GRAY, ANTHONY WHYTE
MARK ANTHONY, K'WAN

STREETS OF NEW YORK VOL. 3
ERICK S GRAY, ANTHONY WHYTE
MARK ANTHONY, TREASURE BLUE

SMUT CENTRAL
BRANDON McCALLA

GHETTO GIRLS
ANTHONY WHYTE

GHETTO GIRLS TOO
ANTHONY WHYTE

**GHETTO GIRLS 3:
SOO HOOD**
ANTHONY WHYTE

**GHETTO GIRLS IV:
YOUNG LUV**
ANTHONY WHYTE

SPOT RUSHERS
BRANDON McCALLA

**IT CAN HAPPEN
IN A MINUTE**
S.M. JOHNSON

LIPSTICK DIARIES
CRYSTAL LACEY WINSLOW
VARIOUS FEMALE AUTHORS

LIPSTICK DIARIES 2
WAHIDA CLARK
VARIOUS FEMALE AUTHORS